GREEK TYCOON, INEXPERIENCED MISTRESS

GREEK TYCOON, INEXPERIENCED MISTRESS

BY

LYNNE GRAHAM

First published in Great Britain 2010
Large Print edition 2010
Harlequin Mills & Boon Limited,
Eton House, 18-24 Paradise Road,
Richmond, Surrey TW9 1SR

© Lynne Graham 2010

ISBN: 978 0 263 21220 4

Harlequin Mills & Boon policy is to use papers that are
natural, renewable and recyclable products and made
from wood grown in sustainable forests. The logging and
manufacturing process conform to the legal environmental
regulations of the country of origin.

Printed and bound in Great Britain
by CPI Antony Rowe, Chippenham, Wiltshire

CHAPTER ONE

As TWO of the more elderly directors of Dionides Shipping again pressed questions that had already been answered Atreus let his attention stray to the Art Deco bronze on the far side of the boardroom. It was of a voluptuous Spanish dancer, only half-clad in what might once have been a romanticised concept of gipsy clothing.

When Atreus had first taken over as CEO of the family business he had been stunned by the sexy statue, which had seemed so out of step with his grandfather's stern, old-fashioned outlook on life.

'She reminded me of my first love,' the old man had confided with a faraway look in his faded eyes. 'She married someone else.'

Atreus could not imagine such a disappointment happening to him. The women he met these days were financially astute and a challenge to shake off. Ever since he'd been a teenager he had been relentlessly hunted by gold-digging beauties who would throw themselves in his path in attempts to ensnare him and his wealth. Black-haired, with eyes dark as sloes, and six foot three inches in height, Atreus had always been an object of desire. By the time he had twice become the unhappy focus of false paternity claims he had decided that he would only marry a woman with a fortune and social standing to match his own. His late father, Achilles, had set his only son a chilling example by living an exemplary life until the age of forty, when he had inexplicably gone off the rails by abandoning his wife and only child to run off with an artist's model famous for dancing on tables. From then on wild self-indulgence and extravagance had ruled the lives of both Atreus's parents, and he had lost his early childhood to their excesses. After that, raised almost entirely by his strict paternal uncle and aunt, Atreus had been deeply suspicious of any inner prompting to step off the straight and narrow. That had been his father's fatal flaw; it would not be his.

Regardless of that fact, the Art Deco bronze had contrived recently to acquire a strange significance for Atreus. It reminded him of an episode some weeks earlier that had taken place on his country estate. On a warm summer afternoon while he had been walking through the woods he had come upon a curvaceous brunette skinny-dipping in the river. Her presence on private land had infuriated him. After all, he had paid a fortune for the seclusion of his large estate, and he employed numerous staff to guard his privacy from trespassers and camera lenses. Ironically, ever since then the memory of the brunette's indescribably lush and creamy curves had had an extraordinarily erotic hold on him—awake and asleep. Yet she had been a woman who had borne not the slightest resemblance to the slender elegant blondes who usually attracted him…

In fact she had not been his type in any way, Atreus acknowledged impatiently. According to his estate manager, Lindy Ryman was an eccentric animal-lover who scratched a living making and selling pot-pourri and candles. A regular churchgoer, she was also a well-respected member of the local community, who hid her remarkable curves beneath drab long skirts and wintry woollens. Atreus had been tough on her in the woods, for at first he had been convinced that she had deliberately schemed—like so many women before her—to set up their encounter. Once he'd appreciated that she was no cunning temptress he had sent her flowers and an apology. He'd been amazed when she'd ignored those olive branches and failed to make use of the phone number he had included.

His mood darkening at the length of time his thoughts had stayed focused on the Ryman woman, Atreus suddenly wondered if he should offer her compensation to surrender her tenancy on his estate. Out of sight would be out of mind, and that might well be the best cure for what afflicted him. He had no doubt that he was too intelligent and logical to succumb to the attraction of a woman who was so outrageously unsuitable for him in every way…

'You dumped Sarah?' Lindy repeated, turning to glance at Ben.

'She was getting serious. Why do women always do that?' Ben enquired, with the pained expression of a male continually tortured by besotted females.

Look in the mirror, Lindy almost told him. She could still recall when she had fallen under the enchantment of Ben's floppy blond hair, light green eyes and rangy frame. That had been way back when they'd first met at university, and he had put her firmly in the pigeonhole marked 'Friends'. There had been no jumping ship. Some of the best days of her life had been wasted while she'd wished that she was tiny, cute and giggly instead of shy, sensible and quiet. Since then Lindy had got over him, and grown accustomed to watching him cut a destructive swathe through a long line of beauties. Ben didn't want commitment, it seemed, just a good time. A City of London trader, he had a successful career and all the worldly trappings that ranged from a flash car to smart suits and the membership of the right gym. Yet Ben never really seemed happy with his lot, Lindy acknowledged ruefully.

'If you weren't as keen as she was, I suppose you were better breaking up with her,' Lindy retorted evenly. Her soft heart went out to Sarah, who had sounded like a pretty nice person and who was probably grieving now over the loss of him—as Lindy had once grieved without even the excuse of ever having had him.

'You are the most fabulous cook.' Ben sighed, taking another bite of her crumbly iced carrot cake and savouring the taste.

Lindy compressed her lips, too well aware

that no such proficiency would ever increase her appeal to the opposite sex. She was convinced that her real problem was that there was too much of her. Ever since she had been likened to a fertility statue at school, and bullied unmercifully on that basis, she had despised her full-breasted, generous-hipped body. Diets and exercise seemed to have little impact, and although she carried no surplus weight anywhere else she was embarrassed by her healthy appetite. Ben always dated small, skinny girls who made Lindy feel enormous and clumsy.

Lindy had dropped out of university when her mother fell ill. An only child from a poor home, she had had to give up studying for a law degree to nurse her mother through a long and sadly terminal decline. On the brink of returning to university Lindy had come down with a nasty bout of glandular fever. By the time she had recovered her own health she had lost interest in studying and had gone for an office job instead. Her flat-sharing days in

London with her friends Elinor and Alissa had been fun, but since then both women had married, moved abroad and had families, so their meetings now were few and far between. Even so, it had been during a summer visit to Elinor and her husband Jasim's English country home that Lindy had first fallen blissfully in love with the countryside. As soon as she had found a rural property at a rent she could afford—The Lodge, a small gatehouse at the edge of a grand estate—she had taken the plunge and jumped off the hamster's wheel of urban working altogether.

Since then Lindy had devoted herself to making a living through pursuits she enjoyed. She grew lavender and roses, and made pot-pourri and candles which sold well via the internet. She took occasional part-time jobs when her bank account needed plumping up, but devoted most of her free time to helping out at the local animal sanctuary. She had acquired two rescue dogs: Samson and Sausage. Her friends might insinuate that she was throwing her youth away, but Lindy was content with her home, her small income and her simple life.

Of course every Eden had to have a serpent, she conceded ruefully. Hers was Atreus Dionides, the new, fabulously wealthy owner of Chantry House, a wonderful Georgian jewel of a mansion surrounded by a beautiful estate. Thanks to him, she was no longer free to roam where she liked through hundreds of acres of parkland and wood. Worst of all, her single unforgettable meeting with the wretched man had humiliated and distressed her so much that she had actually considered moving.

'Are you quite sure that you don't mind looking after Pip?' Ben checked again, on his way out of the front door.

'He'll be fine here.' An essential streak of honesty made Lindy sidestep the question, for if truth be told Pip was far from being her favourite house-guest.

The Chihuahua belonged to Ben's mother, who expected her son to look after her pet whenever she went on holiday. Unhappily, Pip was a very cross little animal. Had he been larger he would have had to wear a muzzle. As it was, the tiny canine continually growled, snapped and barked, and even Lindy's love of dogs was taxed by Pip's bad temper and tendency to bite.

Lindy walked Ben out to his car. 'You shouldn't have parked on the drive. I don't have a parking space here. The estate manager did ask me to ensure that my visitors parked outside the gates,' she reminded him awkwardly.

'The new owner is really making life difficult for you. If he keeps it up, I bet it could constitute harassment,' Ben replied, climbing into the driver's seat and opening the window on the passenger side to continue the conversation.

Lindy tensed and then froze when she saw a long dark limousine gliding through the tall black gates. In a trice, she had dropped down into a crouch by the passenger door, so that she was hidden from view by Ben's sports car.

'What on earth are you doing?' Ben demanded with raised brows.

'Just don't drive off until the limo has gone past!' Lindy hissed, staying down, her face as red as a beetroot and as hot as fire.

The limousine continued down the drive at a stately pace and disappeared round a corner. Lindy slowly rose up to her medium height, glossy dark brown hair rippling round her shoulders, her violet-blue eyes strained and uneasy.

'What were you doing?' Ben asked in a tone of wonderment.

'Never mind.' Lindy shrugged rather unconvincingly. She told Ben she would see him the following Friday, when he came back to pick up Pip, and hurried into her cottage as fast as her legs would carry her, where she found the Chihuahua snarling viciously at poor Sausage, who had taken refuge beneath a chair.

Six weeks had passed since Lindy had met Atreus Dionides, in circumstances that still brought her out in a cold stricken sweat of reluctant remembrance when she strived to adjust to the reality that the Greek shipping tycoon had seen her stark naked. As he was the very first male who had ever seen her in that state, and he had utterly humiliated her, she was still struggling to get over the experience. Had she had the slightest suspicion that anyone might see her she would not have removed so much as a sock in public. After all, she was self-conscious even in a swimsuit, and skinny-dipping wasn't something she had ever done before…or would ever do again in this lifetime.

In fact every time she thought about that afternoon she cringed and cursed her stupidity. On what had turned out to be the hottest day of the year she had spent the morning helping to unload a delivery of hay at the animal sanctuary. Riding home on her bike, her clothes sticking to her overheated skin, she had thought longingly of the river, where the rocks formed a safe natural pool. The previous summer she had paddled there on several occasions.

Of course back then the estate had been

deserted, for it had still belonged to an old man who'd spent most of his time abroad and who had placed no restrictions on his tenants' movements. Atreus Dionides, on the other hand, surrounded himself with high-tech security and knew to the letter of the law what rights he had and what rights his tenants had. The estate office had wasted no time in sending out a letter laying out the new ground rules and stressing the new owner's desire for total seclusion and privacy within his extensive grounds.

But on that hot day six weeks ago Lindy had only intended to cool her bare feet for a few minutes. It was a quiet part of the river, where she had never seen another living soul before and where the trees and shrubs on the banks provided dense cover. Aware that Atreus Dionides usually only used the house at weekends, and that it was midweek, Lindy had succumbed to temptation and impulse and had done something totally out of character. Stripping down to her birthday suit and leaving her clothes in a pile, she had sunk slowly into the pool with a heady sigh of pleasure, revelling in the clean, cold refreshment of the water on her hot damp skin.

'What are you doing here?' an authoritative male voice had demanded, only minutes after her immersion, and she'd very nearly jumped out of her skin in fright.

Whirling round wide-eyed, Lindy had focused on the male poised on the bank and hastily dropped lower in the water to conceal her breasts. Sporting a sophisticated urban black business suit, teamed with a white shirt and silk tie, Atreus had looked bizarre against the backdrop of the natural woodland and all the more unreal. She had known who he was immediately as she had seen his photo when the local newspaper had published an excited article about the new owner of the Chantry estate. Even in black and white newsprint he was a very handsome man, if a little cold and grim in his chilly perfection of features. In person, however, Atreus Dionides was a glowing vision of bronzed masculinity and dark Mediterranean good-looks that would have stopped any woman dead in her tracks.

'This is private property.'

Lindy had crossed her arms in front of her lest the water was not providing sufficient concealment. 'Er... I'm sorry. It won't ever happen again. If you go away I'll get out and get dressed.'

'I'm not moving anywhere,' Atreus had delivered loftily. 'You still haven't told me what you're doing here.'

'It's a hot day. I fancied a swim to cool off,' she'd explained uneasily, while wondering why on earth he felt the need to ask when the answer should have been obvious.

'Stripped, ready and waiting for my first appearance?' the Greek tycoon had retorted with sizzling derision. 'I don't go for naked ladies in the woods, or for brief outdoor encounters. You're wasting your time.'

As it had dawned on Lindy that he actually suspected that she might have whipped off her clothes and got in the water purely in an effort to lure him into some sleazy sexual encounter, she's been so aghast that she'd simply gaped at him in amazement.

'Which of my staff told you I was coming out here?' Atreus Dionides had shot at her.

'Are you always this paranoid?' Lindy had questioned in disbelief. 'Look I'm getting really cold. Move away and I'll get out and be off your land before you know it.'

It had been immediately evident that her reference to paranoia had gone down like a brick thrown through his front window, since he'd pushed back his big wide shoulders and, his aggressive jawline clenched, fixed his dark-as-treacle eyes on her. 'Who tipped you off about my presence here today?'

Her very blue eyes had widened. 'Nobody, I swear. I'm just an ordinary trespasser in the woods—one of your tenants, actually—and I would like to get out of the river and go home now.'

'You're a tenant?' Atreus had queried harshly.

'So, you're trespassing in spite of the estate office's request that you respect my privacy?'

'I live at The Lodge. If I'd known you were at home I'd never have dared,' she'd admitted truthfully, trying and failing to suppress a shiver, because she had only been able to bear the cold water while she was free to move around and jump up and down to keep warm. 'Now, please be a gentleman and return to your…er…walk.'

'The creed of the gentleman is long dead.' He'd produced a mobile phone. 'I'm calling Security to deal with you.'

And that was when Lindy had really lost her head with him. 'How much of a bastard do you have to be? I've said sorry. What more can I do or say? I'm a woman standing naked in freezing water and you're threatening to muster more men to see me like this?' she'd shouted at him in horror. 'I'm very cold, and I want my clothes!'

Hard, dark and unrepentant eyes had rested on her hot, angry face. 'I'm not preventing you from retrieving them.'

And she hadn't been able to wait any longer. By that stage her feet had been so cold she'd been in pain, and she hadn't been able to bear to stand there at his mercy any more. Utterly mortified, and inflamed by his intransigence, she'd waded out without looking anywhere near him. He'd not turned his back as any half-decent man would have done either. He'd stayed where he was and he hadn't apologised. The very fact that no man had ever seen her naked before had made the ordeal that much more painful for her. Unbearably conscious of her bare breasts, and the all too great expanse of the rest of her, almost sick with embarrassment, she'd had to struggle with the difficulty of dragging her jeans and T-shirt over her wet skin. Naturally she hadn't extended the time of her exposure by trying either to dry herself or put on her bra and knickers first.

She'd run all the way back to The Lodge, where she'd sat shell-shocked and tearful over the indignity of the ordeal he had put her through. Forty-eight hours later Atreus Dionides had sent her a superb bouquet of expensive flowers with a card that had contained an apology and the suggestion that she call him to arrange a dinner date. She had not been able to credit his nerve. His insolent invitation had simply sent her into paroxysms of frustrated rage.

Lindy was, after all, quite friendly with his housekeeper, Phoebe Carstairs, and as such was already reasonably well acquainted with his reputation as a womaniser. Phoebe had yet to see her wealthy employer with the same woman twice. According to Phoebe, Atreus liked dainty blondes in very high heels, and they all fawned over him like groupies and slept with him the first night they arrived. Lindy had read between the lines: Atreus was accustomed to a diet of flattery, awe and easy sex, with women capable of amusing him only for a single weekend.

Lindy was not and never would be that kind of a woman. Furthermore, how dared he even suggest that she would want to lay eyes on him again after the brutal, callous way he had treated her? He had shown the true colours of his character by the river. On the surface he might well be everything the newspaper had suggested—a phenomenally brilliant businessman who had taken a failing family company and transformed it into a contemporary Goliath which dominated the world shipping markets. And he was breathtakingly handsome and extraordinarily rich and privileged. But below that lustrous, classically beautiful surface he was a hatefully cold and unfeeling guy, with no manners and a considerable contempt for women. If Lindy had to wait a lifetime to see Atreus Dionides again it would be too soon.

But in fact she was to see Atreus again much sooner than she expected—and in circumstances that would prevent her from expressing her antipathy in the manner she would have liked.

Her bedroom was the only room in her compact gatehouse which provided her with a view of Chantry House. All she could actually see was the west wing of the extensive property, and at present that was not a pretty view because for many weeks that part of the building had been shrouded in unsightly scaffolding while it was being converted into staff accommodation. It was a clear night, without clouds, and when Lindy was closing the curtains shortly before midnight she immediately noticed a puff of smoke issuing from the roof. A frown line dividing her brow, she stared until she saw another, floating up slowly into the night sky. There was no chimney, and nobody living there yet either. She snatched in a dismayed breath, her fingers biting into the curtain as she peered out at the house. She was striving to crush back the bone-deep terror of fire that was already bringing her out in a cold sweat. Could it really be a fire? A suspicion of an orange glow behind a formerly blank window unfroze her from her position. She immediately reached for the phone to call the emergency services.

Then, in a frantic rush, she raced downstairs and snatched up her mobile phone to ring Phoebe Carstairs, who lived in the village and was the sister of Emma, who ran the animal sanctuary.

Phoebe ran out into her garden to take a look at Chantry House from across the fields.

'Oh, my goodness, I can see the smoke from here! We'll have to try and get the house cleared—it's full of priceless furniture and paintings!' Phoebe exclaimed in consternation.

'Phoebe…' Lindy interrupted as the other woman outlined her plan to call in the neighbours to help. 'Is there anyone staying in the house at present?'

'Mr Dionides arrived this afternoon… Oh, yes, and the cat—Dolly. I borrowed her from Emma to catch mice. I'm trying to call Mr Dionides…on the landline right now…but he's not answering. Oh, no, maybe he's been overcome by smoke! Look, you're much closer than I am. You'd better go and knock him up before he gets incinerated in his bed!'

Wincing in reaction at that unfortunate turn of phrase, and suppressing the panic and reluctance awakened by Phoebe's instruction, Lindy fled outside and jumped on her bike. She knew she had no choice but to get involved, and she was determined not to let her fear of fire prevent her from doing what she had to do. She pedalled frantically down the drive. There were no lights on. The mansion looked dead. Letting the bike fall to the gravel, she took the steps to the front door two at a time and hammered as noisily as she could on the giant knocker. Breathless and fiercely concerned, she kept on thumping the knocker until her arm ached and she had to change hands. By the time the big door finally opened, she could hear cars coming up the drive.

'What the hell—? It's after midnight.' Atreus Dionides stared out at her with a frown of incomprehension. He was still fully dressed in an elegant pinstriped suit. With his luxuriant black hair dishevelled and a blue-black shadow of stubble roughening his strong jawline, he was no longer immaculate in appearance, but he looked startlingly masculine and...sexy, Lindy conceded—in some shock at this awareness occurring to her. Her tummy flipped, and perspiration dampened her short upper lip. She was embarrassed for herself.

'The west wing is on fire!' she gasped.

Atreus dealt her a look of frank incredulity. 'What are you talking about?'

'Look, your house is on fire...don't be pigheaded!' Lindy yelled at him, sensing that being obstinate and independent of thought ran through his every fibre, like a name stamped indelibly into a stick of seaside rock.

Atreus strode down the steps. 'On...fire?'

'West wing. Top floor!'

His long, powerful legs cut the distance to the corner of the house at a rate she could not keep up with. Once there, he stilled at the sight of the glow lighting the darkness, while Lindy's tummy gave a sickening lurch and cold fear chilled her to the marrow. A biting

phrase of guttural Greek escaped him before
he was galvanised into action.

Several powerfully built men had already
jumped out of a big four-wheel-drive to race
across the gravel towards him. Lindy recognised the musclebound males who seemed to
travel everywhere with him as his bodyguards.
He rapped out instructions to them and they
walked straight into the house.

'Is it safe to let them go inside?' Lindy
queried worriedly.

'If it were not I would not send them. The
seat of the fire is a considerable distance from
the library,' Atreus responded loftily, his irri-
tation at that suggestion of censure unconcealed. 'My laptop and sensitive papers must
be retrieved.'

Lindy could not credit that he could still be
concentrating solely on business when the
superb paintings she could see decorating the
hall walls were under threat. Didn't he appreciate how terrifyingly fast a fire could move
through a building? A terrifying shiver of re-

membrance that was a powerful hangover from her childhood experiences ran through her. Clenching her hands into fists of restraint, she turned away to approach Phoebe, who was surrounded by a cluster of locals. All of them were frozen into inactivity in the weird fascination of spectators watching a potential disaster develop.

'There's no time to waste. Let's get the artworks out,' Lindy urged.

A chain of willing helpers formed, and the first paintings were removed and passed out through the windows from hand to hand. Lindy, always a talented organiser, co-ordinated the effort, and once the Dionides bodyguards and estate workers joined them the salvage operation began to function with greater speed and efficiency. Two fire engines arrived and Atreus went into immediate consultation with the senior officer in charge. Ladders went up and hoses began to cover the ground. Chantry House sat on a hill, and water would have to be pumped up from the lake if the flames got a firm hold.

The task of clearing valuables from the vast mansion was eased by the fortunate fact that many of the rooms were awaiting redecoration and still empty. As the pressure on the salvage operation lessened Lindy watched in fierce trepidation as jets of water were directed into the burning building and billowing clouds of black smoke poured into the night sky. Even the smell of the smoke in the air made her feel queasy.

'The fire's travelling through the roof void,' Atreus ground out.

'Did the cat get out okay?' Lindy asked, belatedly recalling Dolly, the animal the housekeeper had mentioned.

Atreus urged her back onto the lawn as the orange glare behind a sash window loudly cracked the glass. 'What cat? I don't have animals in the house.'

Lindy dealt him a look of consternation and raced over to Phoebe. A storage lorry was reversing in readiness to load the paintings stacked on the tarpaulins that had been spread on the grass.

'Did Dolly get out?' Lindy asked frantically.

'Oh! I forgot about her!' the older woman admitted guiltily. 'I closed her in the kitchen for the night. I didn't want to risk her getting out and wandering round the house.'

The fire team in the hallway told her she couldn't enter the building. Tears of frustration in her eyes, Lindy pelted round to the back of the house. Would she really have the courage to go inside? she asked herself fiercely, doubting her strength of will in the face of such a challenge? The back door lay open. Her legs felt weak and woolly. She thought about the cat and, sucking in a deep jagged breath, conquered her paralysis and stumbled forward to race into the house. She sped down the flagged corridor and past innumerable closed doors. For a split second she froze in fear, for the smell of the smoke was rousing ever more frightening memories. But commonsense intervened and she snatched up a towel in the laundry room and held it to her face because the acrid smoke was catching horribly at her nose and her throat. Long before she reached the kitchen door, it had become a struggle to breathe.

She could hear a dull roaring sound behind the kitchen door and her courage almost failed to her, but she was powered by an image of Dolly's terror and the sick memory of herself as a child, trapped in a burning house. Using the towel to turn the door handle, in case it was hot, she opened the door just as a man shouted at her from behind.

'Don't open the door...*no!*' he roared, but she was on an adrenalin rush and she did not even turn her head.

She was shaken by the discovery that the ceiling was on fire. Although there was a scattering of small burning pieces of debris on the floor, the kitchen was still eerily intact within that unnatural orange glow of impending destruction. The heat, however, was intense. Dolly had taken shelter under the table. An elderly black and white cat, with big green eyes, she was clearly not her usual placid self. A smouldering piece of wood lay nearby and

Dolly was snarling at it, with her hackles lifted and her fur standing on end.

Lindy surged forward and snatched up Dolly just as the most dreadful rending noise sounded from above her. Inadvertently she paused and obeyed a foolish compulsion to look up. Someone lifted her bodily off her feet and hauled her backwards. A burning beam fell on the table and rolled off again, showering sparks and choking dust only feet away from her. She had been right in its path, and the fear of what might have been hit her hard and left her limp.

Atreus carried Lindy and the struggling cat to safety and withstood a volley of reproof from the fireman who had followed his rescue bid. She was coughing and spluttering as Atreus lowered her to the cobbled yard outside, and she breathed in the clean air with feverish relief.

'How could you be so stupid?' Atreus yelled at her, full volume. 'Why didn't you stop when I shouted at you?'

'I didn't hear you shout!'

'You risked my life and your own for an animal!' Atreus launched at her in condemnation.

That verbal attack shocked her, and at the same moment she feverishly fought disturbing recollections of the household fire that had many years earlier taken her father's life. The combination made her eyes prickle and overflow and she flung him a speaking glance of reproach. 'I couldn't just leave Dolly to die in there!'

The cat was now curled up in Lindy's arms, with her furry head tucked well out of view. She was paying not the smallest heed to the crackling flames leaping through the roof of the west wing, or to the noise and activity of the human beings rushing around. Dolly had had enough excitement for one day and recognised a safe haven when she was offered one.

'You could have been killed or at the very least seriously injured,' Atreus admonished fiercely.

'You were a hero,' Lindy pronounced

through clenched teeth of ingratitude. 'Thank you very much for saving my life.'

Fighting to contain his anger with her, Atreus gazed down at her defiant oval face. She wasn't beautiful but there was something about her, a heady *je ne sais quoi* that made him blatantly aware of her femininity. Was it those clear bright eyes? The luxuriant mane of long dark hair? Or the voluptuous figure that had infiltrated his dreams and caused him more disturbed nights that he cared to remember? She was full of emotion, a far cry from the reserved and controlled women he was used to dealing with. Her tear-filled eyes were as bright as amethysts, her lush, vulnerable mouth as ripe as a peach, and she continued to tremble as if the fire was still overhead. Anger lurched inexplicably into more complex responses that tensed his big powerful frame with surprise and electric sexuality. Hunger for her hit him as hard as a punch in the gut.

'I know I don't sound grateful,' Lindy added

gruffly, staring up at him, striving not to notice how beautifully his thick black lashes enhanced his stunning dark golden eyes. 'But I am really. Dolly was so frightened—didn't you see her?'

'*Nasi pari o Diavelos*,' Atreus swore raggedly under his breath. '*I saw only you.*'

His intensity slashed through her strained attempt to behave normally. Her mouth running dry in the tension-filled atmosphere, she collided with his smouldering gaze and her ability to breathe seized up. He swooped like the predator she sensed he was at heart. He did not ask, he simply took, and his wide sensual mouth engulfed hers with a hot, driving energy that sizzled through her unprepared body like flame consuming tinder-dry wood. She moaned at the penetration of his tongue between her lips and the slow, sensual glide of it against hers, because her body was going haywire.

Sultry heat was tingling through her nerve-endings in a seductive wave. She tried to make herself pull back from him but could not find sufficient will-power to contrive that feat of mind over matter. Her nipples were lengthening into pointed pulsing buds constrained by the lace cups of her bra, and there was a treacherous yearning burn and an embarrassing dampness between her thighs. Together those sensations were winding her up as tight as a clock spring. As he pressed her against him, even through the barrier of their clothes, she was hopelessly aware of the hard, thrusting evidence of his arousal.

'Full marks for surprising me,' Atreus said huskily, surveying her with bold appreciation as he tilted back his handsome head. 'You are hotter than that fire in there, *mali mou.*'

Lindy, who had never seen herself as being hot in any capacity, sucked oxygen into her depleted lungs and accidentally, in her eagerness to avoid Atreus's scrutiny, caught the eye of the woman who had taken up a hesitant stance several feet away. It was Phoebe Carstairs.

'I'm sorry for interrupting, Mr Dionides,'

the older woman said awkwardly. 'But I thought I could take care of the cat for you.'

On wobbly lower limbs, Lindy detached herself from Atreus and moved away to hand over the cat, who had tolerated being crushed between their straining bodies without complaint. She could not meet Phoebe's eyes; she was in shock…

CHAPTER TWO

'WE CAN make tea, coffee and sandwiches at The Lodge,' Lindy told Phoebe only minutes later, whipping herself straight back into her sensible self and suppressing all memory of that temporary slide into a persona and behaviour alien to her. 'Everyone will need a break and my house is the most convenient. I have to get my bike. If you have nothing more pressing to do, follow me down in your car.'

But even back within the cosy confines of her safe home Lindy discovered that she couldn't stop her hands shaking. She might have mastered her thoughts, but her body was still caught up in shock. She leant up against the sink, breathing in and out in steadying streams. She had gone into the house and got

Dolly. That was all that mattered. She hadn't let her terror of fire paralyse her as it had threatened to do, she reminded herself soothingly. She was not the hysterical type. She was not. She would leave the past where it belonged and stay calm. There would be no crying or silly fussing. The deed was done and nobody had got hurt.

Slowly her hands began to steady and she felt in control again. That reminded her that for a timeless instant in the circle of the Greek tycoon's arms she had felt frighteningly out of control. Of course the fire had roused distressing fragments of memory which had knocked her very much off balance. How silly she had been, clinging to him like that! But these days what was in a kiss? she asked herself in exasperation. In the press, kisses had become almost meaningless in the face of far more intimate embraces, and in the literal heat of the moment were men not more prone to such physical reactions?

It hadn't meant anything—of course it hadn't.

It was just that they were both shaken up and rejoicing in being alive and unharmed. Goodness, she wasn't Atreus Dionides's type at all! She wasn't small, blonde and beautiful, or even wellgroomed. Lindy glanced down at the corduroy skirt and V-necked sweater she wore and a rueful peal of laughter parted her lips. The kiss had just been one of those crazy inexplicable things and she would soon forget about it....

But she would not forget how he had made her feel. No, indeed. It would take total amnesia to wipe out the memory of that jaggedly sweet pleasure—jagged because it hurt to feel anything that strong and sweet, because it had melted every bone in her body and dissolved her self-discipline. No other guy had ever managed a feat like that. In fact, never until now had Lindy realised what all the fuss was about when it came to sex. She might not yet have met a man she wanted to sleep with, but she had certainly kissed plenty of frogs in her time. By no stretch of the imagination was

Atreus a frog, but that had no bearing on the fact that he was as out of her reach as an astronaut on the moon.

Phoebe finally arrived with a laundry basket packed with provisions. The owner of the village shop had opened up specially to sell her bread and cooked meats, and had donated a pile of paper cups. The two women set about making trays of sandwiches.

'Lindy?' Phoebe said tautly, breaking the companionable silence. 'Please don't be offended, but I feel I should warn you to be careful with Mr Dionides. I have every respect for him as my employer, but I can't help having noticed that he's a very smooth operator with women. I don't think he takes any of them seriously.'

'The kiss was a flash in the pan—one of those daft things that just happens in the heat of the moment,' Lindy responded in a dismissive tone of faked amusement. 'I don't know what came over either of us, but it won't be happening again.'

'I would hate to see you getting led down the garden path,' the housekeeper confided in a more relaxed tone.

'I'm very resilient and not given to flights of fancy,' Lindy countered.

And she reminded herself of those facts when Atreus himself put in an appearance an hour later. She saw him across the crush in her small packed living room where, to find a space, people stood or sat on the arms of chairs, or even lounged back against the walls. Atreus was unmissable because he towered over everyone else, his dark well-shaped head instantly visible. He was talking on a mobile phone, the shadow of stubble outlining his masculine jaw line heavier than before. He had fabulous bone structure, from the defined width of his proud cheekbones divided by his arrogant blade of his nose to the unsettling fullness of his wide, sensual mouth.

She had to drag her attention from his hard, handsome face to notice that there was a long rip in the sleeve of his jacket, and the cuffs and front of his shirt were smoke-stained. She wondered with a stab of concern if he had got hurt. She glimpsed the glimmering gold of his stunning eyes as he frowned, ebony brows pleating, and she ducked back into the kitchen before he could see her. Even after that brief exposure her heart was already hammering as fast as if she'd run a marathon. He was gorgeous—there was no other word to better describe him. Instant exhilaration and renewed energy leapt and bounded through her, banishing her weariness, overpowering any sensible train of thought.

'More tea?' Phoebe prompted.

'No. I think the rush is over.' As the kitchen door opened Lindy swivelled, and when she saw who it was she felt ridiculously like a schoolgirl being confronted by a grown-up who knew she had a huge crush on him.

'So this is where you are,' Atreus drawled. 'Come into the other room.'

'I'm really busy—'

'You're a hive of industry, a very capable

woman. I'm impressed, but it's time you relaxed,' he intoned, closing a dominant hand over hers and tugging her willy-nilly back to the door where he stood.

Never comfortable in receipt of praise, Lindy frowned. 'I didn't do anything that other people didn't do.'

'You organised them all. I saw you in action. You're a remarkably bossy little thing,' Atreus remarked with unhidden amusement.

Nobody had ever described Lindy as 'little'. But then he was very tall, and in comparison to him she supposed that she could be considered small. Her fingers trembled in the hold of his. After those unexpected compliments she could hardly catch her breath, never mind speak. They were on the threshold of the living room. Heads turned in their direction and stayed turned at the sight of them poised there together. Her creamy skin flamed. She saw the speculative looks they were attracting and averted her gaze.

'It doesn't take much to encourage gossip round here,' she warned him ruefully.

'Does that bother you? Conventional women don't strip and jump into rivers in broad daylight,' Atreus countered.

Lindy froze. 'I still haven't forgiven you for the way you behaved that day.'

Atreus was not accustomed either to seeking forgiveness or indeed absolution. Women invariably made life easy for him by affecting not to notice his mistakes or omissions. Last-minute cancellations and his appearances in the company of other women were always ignored to ensure that he called again. He had learned that when it came to her sex he could get away with just about anything.

'You were a real seven-letter-word that day at the river!' Lindy proclaimed without hesitation, when he made no comment.

Atreus tried to recall when he had last heard anyone utilise such care to avoid a swear-word and he was amused.

'You were rude, thoroughly unpleasant and unreasonable, and you humiliated me!' Lindy spelt out in a fiery rush to get her point across.

'I apologised to you,' Atreus reminded her, with more than a touch of impatience. 'I rarely apologise.'

It was true that he had apologised, Lindy acknowledged ruefully, wondering if she was being unfair in still holding spite. After all, the man had saved her from serious injury when she'd rescued Dolly. He had also proved that in a crisis he was cool, courageous and protective, all sterling qualities of character which she very much admired. So why couldn't she escape the suspicion that treating a woman well didn't come naturally to Atreus Dionides?

'I don't know why you're flirting with me,' she told him flatly.

'Don't you?'

The doubt in his tone provoked her into looking up, and she met smouldering golden eyes below the black sweep of his lashes. Excitement hurtled through her like a wild wake-up call. Thought and breath were suspended. Without any warning at all she wanted his mouth so badly on hers that being denied it hurt. In shock, she tore her gaze from his and retreated into the kitchen.

A split second later all the lights in the house went out. A buzz of dismayed comment was accompanied by the sound of switches being put on and off without success. The kitchen door opened.

'Your electricity supply must be connected to that of Chantry House, which has been disconnected for safety.' Atreus's accented drawl came out of the darkness. 'It'll take some time to reorganise that, and it's unlikely to be today.'

'Oh, great,' Lindy muttered ruefully, leaning back against the kitchen cupboards and pushing her dark hair off her damp brow. The shower she had been dreaming about was out of reach now.

The locals began to leave with a chorus of thank-yous for her hospitality.

'You go as well, Phoebe,' Lindy urged the Chantry housekeeper, who was hovering at her elbow. 'It's been a long night and there's no need for you to stay on. Most of the cleaning up has already been done.'

'If you're sure?' Phoebe said uncertainly.

'Of course I am.'

'Why don't you come home with me?' the older woman asked. 'At least we have electricity.'

'We're not that far away from dawn. I'll be okay,' Lindy pointed out, reckoning that her companion, who had five children and a husband packed into her tiny terraced house, had quite enough people to contend with when she got home. She groped below the sink to locate her torch, and lit Phoebe's departure through the back door, locking up in the older woman's wake.

'Lindy?'

Lindy flinched in surprise at the sound of the Greek tycoon's distinctive accented drawl, travelling from the room next door. 'I thought you'd already gone,' she admitted, able to distinguish now between different shades of light and dark and picking out his tall, dark silhouette by the living room window.

'Some thanks that would be for the assistance you gave tonight—abandoning you here without either power or heating,' Atreus derided. 'I have a suite booked at Headby Hall and I'd like you to come with me.'

'I couldn't possibly,' Lindy breathed, taken aback by that casual invitation to the leading country house hotel for miles around.

'Don't be impractical. You must be as eager for a shower and a break as I am,' he pointed out. 'In little more than four hours I have to be back at the house to meet the insurance assessors and the conservation team being put together as we speak.'

'I'll be fine here,' she asserted.

'You would genuinely prefer to sit here unwashed and cold rather than accompany me to a more civilised and comfortable location?'

Her small white teeth set together hard, because he was making her sound peculiar while at the same time his tone somehow contrived to suggest that such standoffish behaviour was only what he had expected from her all along. 'Give me a couple of minutes to pack a bag,' she told him, her voice as abrupt as the decision she had reached.

By the light of the torch she flung pyjamas and a change of clothes into an overnight bag. The dogs had food, water and cosy kennels, and although they were accustomed to sleeping indoors with her they would be all right until the morning. Even so, she was belatedly stunned that she could have agreed to go to a hotel with Atreus Dionides, for such bold behaviour didn't come naturally to her.

Lindy eased into the back of the limousine with as much cool as she could muster. In the act of regretting her agreement, she turned to address Atreus—but his phone was already ringing again and his attention was elsewhere. She listened to him talking in what she assumed to be Greek and asked herself why she should feel so apprehensive. After all, he was only being kind in offering her an escape from a cold, dark house without hot water.

Headby Hall was the ultimate in luxury hotels, and Lindy had never crossed its threshold before. She was horribly conscious of her humble clothing and severely tried by Atreus's efforts to get her to walk through the foyer ahead of him when what she most wanted was to reach the lift without being noticed by a single living soul.

'Aren't you tired?' she asked him in wonderment when he completed yet another phone call.

'I'm still operating on adrenaline.'

'I'm sorry about the house. I know that the work you were having done was almost complete.'

'I have other houses,' he asserted.

Without thinking, Lindy rested a light hand on his arm. 'I noticed the rip in your jacket. Did you get hurt?' she asked anxiously.

Atreus looked down into her warm, sympathetic gaze and wondered when a woman had last looked at him as if she was restraining a powerful need to offer him comfort and a hug. Never, he acknowledged wryly, not even when he had been a child. In his experience women were usually more gifted at taking, and there was a hefty price ticket attached to anything on offer with any greater depth.

'It's only a scratch.'

Meeting his brilliant dark golden eyes, she felt her mouth run dry and her tummy lurched. The lift doors opened and she stiffened and tore her gaze from his. They walked down a private corridor to a door that was already being opened by a member of his staff. Tense with unease, Lindy entered a splendid, sumptuously furnished reception room adorned with fresh flowers. Designer luggage was being carried into one bedroom while her ancient holdall was already comfortingly visible through the doors of a second.

'I've ordered some food for us. You didn't eat anything while I was around,' Atreus remarked.

'I'll get changed,' Lindy muttered, heading for the second bedroom with alacrity.

In the *en suite* bathroom, she stripped where she stood and used the hotel toiletries to wash her hair and freshen up in the shower. It was wonderful to rinse away the smell of smoke that seemed to have impregnated her skin and everything she wore. Clean again, she dried her hair with the dryer provided, using her fingers and then fetched her clothes from the holdall. She donned a long green skirt and a cream T-shirt, and left her legs and feet bare because she couldn't face struggling into tights or shoes. She grimaced at her reflection in the mirror, for her glossy dark brown hair had fallen into the natural waves she disliked and she was convinced that her face was as pink as a freshly scrubbed lobster.

A trolley of food now stood beside the table and chairs in the reception room next door. Atreus was waiting for her and, like her, he had opted for informality. His black hair was damp and swept back from his lean, darkly handsome features. He was wearing black designer jeans and an open-necked shirt. As she appeared he studied her for a long moment and then slowly smiled.

And that smile on his wide, sensual mouth lit Lindy up inside like the blazing fire that had devoured a good third of Chantry House. It left little room for anything but instant reaction on all fronts. Her face was hot, and she sat down because she felt dizzy. Eyes screened by her lashes, she surveyed him, from his straight brows and dark deepset eyes to his newly shaven jawline, no longer defined by a blue-black shadow of stubble. There was something about the exact arrangement of his arrestingly beautiful features that drew her more than mere good-looks, she acknowledged in a daze. He magnetised her, exuding an irresistible pull of energy that overwhelmed her usual common sense. Sexual attraction had never hit her so hard.

Lindy accepted a couple of snacks and nibbled at them without much appetite while Atreus talked about the meetings he already had lined up for the morning. Even the sound of his voice set up a responsive vibration in her backbone. When she met his eyes she felt as if the ground had vanished and she was in mid-air, in the act of falling from a great height. It was terrifying and exhilarating and, because such excessive sensations were previously unknown to her, she decided that feeling that way around him was wrong and dangerous.

Indeed, as soon as an opportunity offered itself Lindy rose to her feet and smoothed damp palms down over her skirt. 'I'm very tired. I think I'll turn in now. Thanks for supper…and the shower was very welcome,' she added with a warm smile.

And just like that she was gone.

Atreus studied the closed door of her bedroom in amazement and wondered when he had last run into a brick wall put up by a woman flatly refusing to acknowledge or respond to his signals. Never. He was torn between amusement and frustration.

Lindy leant briefly up against the back of the door and tried to be proud of her self-restraint.

She had resisted him, the most beautiful sexually compelling male she had ever met. She was still stunned that he had found her attractive. Or had it simply been a matter of her being the only woman available for a little dalliance after a stressful day? Was that her putting herself down again? Whatever, she had no doubt that he had had every intention of their ending what remained of the night in the same bed.

That would have been a very foolish move on her part, she told herself ruefully. The idea of a one-night stand with a man she hardly knew filled her with distaste. On the other hand, a little voice she didn't recognise murmured inside her head, he might well have been a once-in-a-lifetime experience. Or was that wishful thinking? She was ashamed of the way her mind was working. She had never planned to be a virgin at her age; it was just something that had happened when a serious relationship failed to transpire. Atreus was pretty much the first man to seriously attract her since those first heady days in Ben's radius. Of course she was curious about sex, but that was not an excuse to conduct an experiment. If she had been embarrassed when he'd seen her naked in the river, how would she feel meeting him in future if she had shared a bed with him?

With a shudder of reaction at that mortifying thought, Lindy embraced her cautious, sensible self and climbed into bed naked, enjoying the cool feel of the sheets against her bare skin. She had never been so tired in her life, but she still felt very jumpy and found it hard to relax—even though her limbs felt like lead weights on the comfortable mattress. She set her mobile phone alarm to rouse her at eight and mentally counted sheep. Within minutes she was sliding into a deep sleep. Her dreams, however, were very far from being soothing. Too many disturbing memories had been unleashed by the fire, and all her rigorous attempts to suppress those upsetting images while she was still awake had failed to lay them to rest.

'Lindy…wake up!' She fought through the barriers of sleep and realised that her shoulder was being shaken.

She sat up with a start, her eyes flying open not on the scary scene which had been unfolding behind her lowered eyelids but on a lamplit and momentarily unfamiliar room. Bewildered, and very distressed by what she had recalled, she only then processed the reality that she was shaking and sobbing.

'You were dreaming. You're awake now,' Atreus asserted, sitting down on the edge of the bed. Bare-chested, he had clearly only paused to pull on his jeans before coming in.

As Atreus entered her field of vision Lindy belatedly acknowledged his presence and stiffened in alarm. 'Did I wake you up?'

'You were screaming at the top of your voice. That must have been some bad dream,' Atreus responded, his attention roaming to the ripe swell of her full breasts which were only just covered by the sheet and resolutely shifting upward again.

A violent shudder rippled through Lindy. 'Because it wasn't a dream,' she shared, on the back of another heaving sob. 'When I was f-four years old, I was in a house fire.'

Atreus tensed, frowning while he watched the tears drip off her chin and listening to her sniff. She was really crying, and not in a cute way either, for her nose had turned pink and her eyelids were swollen. But there was something extraordinarily touching about her genuine distress, and he closed an arm round her in an abrupt and almost clumsy movement.

It was one of those very rare occasions in life when Atreus felt out of his depth. Being supportive didn't come naturally to him. He had grown up in a family famed for its reserve and formality. He had been taught to avoid emotion like the plague and he had no close ties with his surviving relatives. He had never had a serious relationship with a woman, and had always walked away when an affair threatened to become complicated.

The warmth of his arm was comforting.

Lindy struggled to control the sobs and the tempest of emotion still rising inside her. 'Afterwards, my mum told me that my dad must've fallen asleep with a cigarette in his hand and the sofa caught fire. He'd been drinking—my mum was in hospital. I woke up and there was smoke coming under the door and a funny smell,' she related shakily.

Atreus swore half under his breath in Greek. 'And yet you went into a burning house to save a cat tonight?' he breathed, in wrathful incredulity.

Lindy's mind was still firmly lodged in past events. 'I tried to go downstairs but I could see something was in flames at the foot. I was terrified, so I started screaming for Dad.' Her voice cut off, and she twisted and buried her face in the warm living flesh of Atreus's bronzed shoulder. 'For a moment I saw him, but until tonight I didn't remember that I had actually seen him. He was trying to come to me but the fire got him!' she sobbed brokenly.

Atreus was appalled. A dark frown stamping

his features, he wrapped his other arm round her shuddering body and held her close. He was thinking about the selfless way she had rushed to the fire at Chantry House and helped out in every way she could. Not by a word or even a gesture had she hinted at what that intervention must have cost her emotionally. 'You're a very brave woman, *mali mou*.'

'I'm just ordinary.' Lindy snatched in a sustaining breath and choked back another sob, fighting with all her might to get a grip on her flailing emotions. 'I don't know why I'm crying now about something that happened so long ago.' '

'The fire at Chantry last night brought it all to the surface again. How did you escape when you were a child?'

'I believe a fireman rescued me, but I don't remember it. I was incredibly lucky to survive.' Her voice petered out in shock as she finally registered that the sheet between them had slipped. Her bare breasts were crushed against his hair-roughened masculine torso. 'I'm so sorry I woke you up.'

'You didn't. I couldn't sleep,' Atreus admitted, long lean fingers lacing into the tousled tumble of her dark hair to turn her face up.

Smouldering dark golden-brown eyes assailed hers, and then he brought his handsome mouth down and captured her lips with a piercingly sweet eroticism that cut through her defences like a knife. Breathing in little fractured bursts, Lindy drowned in those hungry, drugging kisses, her body quickening and heating in response. There was a frantic driving edge to every sensation: the stingingly tight sensitivity of her nipples, the tugging pull of dissatisfaction at the heart of her.

Atreus closed his hands round the creamy magnificence of her jutting breasts and moulded them with a husky masculine sound of satisfaction. He used his thumbs to chafe the quivering pink tips until, in pursuit of closer contact, he pressed her back against the pillows and put his mouth to her breast instead.

A gasp was dragged from Lindy, who was reeling in sensual shock from the impact of his lovemaking. The tug of his lips and his teeth, and the brush of his tongue on her torment- ingly sensitive nipples, made her squirm while desire flared ever higher and stronger inside her. That she had to struggle even to think straight, however, scared her.

'We hardly know each other!' she protested.

'This is the very best way to get to know me, *glikia mou*,' Atreus intoned with conviction

'But I didn't want to get to know you!' Lindy objected, guiltily studying the clinging fingers she had knotted into the springy depths of his black hair.

'You want me and I want you. Why should that be a problem?'

'Because it is… I don't do stuff like this.'

'You don't have to do anything,' Atreus declared with single-minded purpose.

'You're not my type,' she told him in des- peration.

'Why didn't you say so sooner?' Atreus levered back from her to gaze down at her with shimmering golden eyes full of enquiry.

Lindy crossed concealing arms over her breasts.

'I love looking at you,' Atreus confided, stroking an appreciative hand down to the point where her surprisingly small waist segued into the violin curve of her hip. 'You have the most spectacular shape.'

The intensity of his appraisal convinced her of his sincere approbation and lessened her discomfiture. Without being aware of any prompting to do so, Lindy slowly, shyly parted her arms again, because she was discovering that she really loved the idea of him looking at her and admiring her. Not a single compliment on that score had ever come Lindy's way. Until that moment her voluptuous curves had been a physical flaw and an embarrassment which she hid to the best of her ability. But, transfixed by the glow of bold appreciation in Atreus's gaze, she felt like a goddess come to earth to mesmerise mortal man.

'You looked at the riverbank,' Lindy accused him.

'*Ise omorfi*... you are beautiful…of course I did. The glory of you took my breath away, *mali mou*.'

He had barely finished speaking before Lindy stretched up and sought his wide, sensual mouth for herself again. She savoured the taste of him like a precious wine, parting her lips eagerly for the erotic plunge of his tongue while she quivered at the clenching tightness of response low in her pelvis. He had ignited a hunger in her that she could not resist.

'Is this a yes?'

'Yes…'Lindy whispered, feeling madly daring and sexy for the first time in her life while she defied the voice of restraint and reproach striving to be heard in the back of her head.

The pressure of his mouth on hers was an enticement of no mean order. Her head fell back against the pillows, her neck extending in a soundless sigh as he touched her where she had never been touched before. Little tremors of fierce response assailed her while he teased the honeyed folds of flesh between her thighs. The pleasure was exquisite, but as her excitement grew the pleasure came closer to sensual torture. The more he touched her, the more she wanted, and the less she wanted to wait. He suckled the distended peaks of her breasts and her spine arched, and she cried out as he probed the narrow passage at the swollen heart of her.

She was dimly aware of him removing his jeans and a moment of panic claimed her. 'Don't get me pregnant...' she warned him. 'I'm not using anything.'

'That's not a risk I would ever take,' Atreus imparted, donning protection and hauling her back to him with impatient hands. 'I want you so much it hurts.'

'Will it hurt?' Lindy pressed awkwardly.

A look of bemusement clouded his smouldering gaze. 'Why should it hurt?'

'I haven't done this before...I just wondered.'

Atreus studied her with frowning intensity. 'I will be the first?'

Her body tingling, her face burning, Lindy nodded.

Atreus groaned out loud, recognising the anxiety in her violet-blue eyes, acknowledging that she continually managed to surprise him. 'I'll be very gentle, *glikia mou,*' he swore—he a man who had never tried to be gentle before.

And he was: coaxing and teasing her responsive body until she was on fire with wanting him. She waited in an agony of anticipation and desire for the moment when he eased his rock-hard shaft into the velvet-soft sheath of her womanhood. She saw pleasure score his lean, hard features and marvelled at the extraordinary sense of intimacy a split second before a sharp pain provoked her into venting a cry of dismay.

He stopped, talked to her in husky Greek, kissed her until she relaxed again. And then it went on, the slow, deep penetration that made her gasp and moan with increasing fervour and excitement while he arched her up to receive him and plunged back into her again.

Suddenly she was riding a high of erotic sensation, out of control and abandoned to the wild need he had incited. The orgasm, when it came, took her by surprise and stunned her, before the irresistible waves of shuddering physical satisfaction took over.

'You were amazing,' Atreus told her with a blazing smile of approbation.

'So were you,' Lindy whispered, feverishly trying to suppress the screaming fit of self-doubt, shame and incredulity ready to pounce on her. She wrapped her arms around him and kissed him, fighting the lingering shards of doubt and regret as hard as she could. She found him amazingly attractive and had acted on it, she told herself staunchly. There was no point beating herself up about what could not be changed.

Taken aback though he was by that affectionate kiss, and what has undeniably been a hug, Atreus still tugged her back to him when she attempted to back away. 'I can't wait until the next time, *mali mou*.'

Her eyes widened.

'I don't do one-night-stands,' he told her in reproof.

'Don't you?' Discomfiture was beginning to claim her, for she was feeling very much out of her depth.

A slashing grin curved his beautiful mouth. 'And neither do you…'

CHAPTER THREE

SAMSON and Sausage gave Lindy a rapturous welcome when she returned home, while Pip picked at his food and snarled whenever the other dogs came within yards of his feeding bowl. Awesomely conscious of Atreus waiting impatiently indoors for her, Lindy ignored her usual tasks and went straight back inside with her pets in tow.

Samson, a Jack Russell terrier with perky ears and a cheerful propensity to treat everyone like a long-lost best friend, went straight over to greet Atreus. Sausage hung back, while Pip put on a burst of speed and, barking furiously, raced straight over to the interloper and sank his teeth into his trouser leg. Samson started to bark as well and, aghast,

Lindy waded in, urging peace on all parties while she strove to detach Pip from his glowering victim.

'I'm so sorry. He's a very bad-tempered dog. Thank you for not kicking him away.' Lindy removed a snarling Pip and then gasped, 'Oh, my goodness he's lost one of his teeth!'

'Is it embedded in my leg?' Atreus asked.

'No, it's lying here on the carpet,' Lindy answered, deaf to his tone of irony. She peered into the cross little Chihuahua's mouth and was shocked by the sight of his swollen gums. 'I never realised he had such bad teeth. He must be in a lot of pain. Poor little thing.'

While Lindy soothed and quieted the canine attacker with copious sympathy, Atreus fumed in silence. He had never had anything to do with dogs, and now he had been bitten by one in circumstances guaranteed to bolster his repugnance. 'Are you coming up to the house with me?'

Lindy froze, violet eyes locking to his lean,

darkly handsome face. 'I would rather not draw attention to our…er…new…er…'

As her voice trailed off without her finding an appropriate word, Atreus stepped in. 'Intimacy?'

The word struck Lindy like a brick and she paled, guilt looming large, for the word seemed richly redolent of beds and tumbled sheets— imagery that assailed her conscience like a panic attack. 'Yes. I don't want anyone to know.'

That was not a request Atreus had ever received before. Women usually wanted to show off their association with him, not hide it. But he had always had a high regard for discretion and prudence. The Dionides family were, after all, famous for their dislike of publicity. Birth, marriage and death, and occasional references in the business press, were unavoidable exceptions for so very rich a family. But beyond that level Atreus and his relatives shunned public notice and abhorred the brash, extravagant lifestyle of the celebrity world.

'I'll be very discreet,' he assured her. 'We'll

see each other at weekends, when I come down here.'

Lindy studied him with perplexed eyes, for she could not yet accept that they could be a couple in any way, never mind a couple with an ongoing relationship.

'We've got nothing in common,' she pointed out.

'Differences are stimulating,' Atreus traded smoothly, averting his attention from the little rat-like dog baring its crooked teeth at him from the shelter of her arms before she put it through to the kitchen. The Jack Russell had dropped a rubber bone expectantly at his feet, while the short hairy one was fussing beside a chair and for some reason regarding him with equal anticipation. Atreus decided to spell out his feelings: 'I'm not into pets—particularly indoors.'

'I suppose you didn't have any when you were a child,' Lindy responded, giving him a huge look of sympathy and not one whit perturbed by his loaded statement. 'That's such a shame. But you'll soon get used to my pets.'

She was trying to imagine seeing him at weekends, slotting him into her ordinary activities and failing abysmally to rise to the challenge. Even the idea of him becoming a part of her life struck her as astonishing. 'I don't know why you want to see me again.'

Atreus was bewildered by a response which had never come his way before. A faint stab of guilt assailed him because her lack of vanity and pure likeability shone from her. She was not at all like his usual lovers, he acknowledged wryly. She didn't know the rules he played by and she would probably get hurt. He recalled the total lack of cool and control she displayed when she hugged him and he almost winced. But she would eventually learn, he reasoned steadily, squaring his broad shoulders.

She would have to learn—because he would not contemplate not seeing her again. The bottom line was that he wanted her in his life. Obviously he was ready for a change, for something different, and she would be a breath of fresh air. She was strong, discreet and honest, qualities which he valued highly and which were hard to find in her sex. He would relax with her at weekends, stepping back from the long, stressful hours he worked and the boring social occasions. He met her bewildered violet-blue eyes and realised that if anything he wanted her even more powerfully than he had some hours earlier. The strength of his desire made him uneasy, but it also propelled him forward to ease her into his arms.

Always more comfortable with the physical than the emotional, Atreus lowered his arrogant dark head and brought his mouth down on hers with passionate urgency. That kiss was like an electric shock, first stunning Lindy and then spreading tingling waves of reaction through her. The pressure of his lips and the plunging penetration of his tongue jolted her and made very fibre of her body sing with sexual awareness. Her nipples tightened, her tummy flipped, and looking up into his smouldering dark golden eyes left her dizzy.

'I want to take you back to bed,' he admitted

in a raw undertone of frustration, both hands splayed on her hips to hold her close enough to feel the hard male heat of his arousal. 'Once was very far from being enough.'

Lindy reddened, struggling with the notion of herself as some sort of temptress but loving it—and the proof of it in his physical reaction to her too.

'Unfortunately I have a meeting up at the house,' he reminded her.

'Several,' she told him with a smile.

'Either come with me or go back to the hotel. You can do nothing here without electricity.'

'I may not be able to make candles, but I can cut lavender and make pot pourri,' she contradicted.

'But you don't have to do any of that right now.'

The bell at the front door buzzed.

Lindy peered out of the window and saw her friend's car. 'It's Ben,' she said.

'Ben?' Atreus queried, moving to the window to note the BMW parked on the drive.

'A good friend of mine. He's here to collect Pip, the little dog that nipped you. Pip belongs to his mother,' she explained.

Ben strode straight into the hall. 'I'm on a day off so I thought I'd come down early. It interferes less with my social life,' he confided, with a speaking roll of his eyes.

Lindy launched right into telling him about Pip's swollen gums. She urged him to take the little animal to his mother's vet for a check-up. 'Painful teeth could explain why he's so cross. He needs treatment urgently,' she stressed. 'I'll go and get him for you.'

'Aren't you inviting me in?' But Ben was talking to thin air, because Lindy had already hurried off to slot Pip into his travelling basket.

'Where did the limo outside come from?' Ben called in her wake.

A split second after Lindy returned with the basket Atreus appeared on the threshold of the sitting room. 'It's mine—'

Lindy introduced the two men with a pro-nounced casualness that brought a gleam to

Atreus's dark watchful gaze. Ben recognised the name at once, and immediately adopted a more businesslike manner.

'Chantry House almost burnt down last night. A crowd of us helped to clear up,' Lindy explained.

'But Lindy offered the most valuable assistance,' Atreus imparted.

Lindy stiffened in surprise when Atreus curved a light arm to her spine. Ben noticed, and sent her a frowning questioning glance. Her cheeks burned.

'I'd like to take you out for lunch as thanks for putting up with Pip,' Ben announced.

'Unfortunately Lindy is already booked,' Atreus breathed silkily.

'Sorry,' Lindy muttered, wondering why on earth Ben should have suddenly invited her out for a meal and then understanding as she picked up on the bristling attitude between the two men: Ben was curious. She felt like a bone between two dogs, and was thoroughly irritated, both by Ben's unprecedented invitation and Atreus's arrogant assumption that his last-minute invitation would take priority with her. But it did take priority, she conceded ruefully, even if she disliked his methods.

'I'll call you later,' Ben told her stiffly.

'No, you can't leave yet. I'll make coffee for us.'

His stunning dark eyes cool as ice water, Atreus opened the front door. 'I'll pick you up at twelve.'

'What the blazes are you playing at with that guy?' Ben demanded within seconds of the door shutting in the Greek tycoon's wake.

Lindy was tempted to tell Ben to mind his own business, and had to remind herself that close friends were entitled to ask awkward questions.

'He's been flirting with me…that's all,' she replied lightly, finding it quite impossible to even consider telling Ben the truth.

'Of course that's all,' Ben agreed with wounding conviction. 'I would very much doubt that you have what it takes to tempt Atreus Dionides into anything more. He's a billionaire shipping tycoon and he only dates stunningly beautiful women.'

'Coffee,' Lindy pronounced through clenched teeth, resisting the humiliating urge to tell Ben that while he might not find her attractive Atreus certainly did.

Ben didn't stay long, because Lindy wanted time to get dressed for lunch. He was not as relaxed with her as he usually was, and she wondered if it was insane of her to suspect that the suggestion that another man might be interested in her had thoroughly irritated her platonic friend.

Lindy put on the smartest outfit in her wardrobe—an elegant black trouser suit. Atreus had let his bodyguard come to the door for her, and when she got into the limousine he treated her to a thirty-second appraisal before saying, 'I prefer skirts on women.'

'Do you?' Lindy bridled at that untimely comment. 'Am I supposed to write that down in a little black book and never wear trousers again?'

'Where does Ben fit in?' Atreus enquired, neatly sidestepping her tart response.

Lindy gave him a puzzled frown and then laughed. 'I thought he was the love of my life when I was a student of eighteen, but unfortunately, he didn't see me in the same light. I got over him, we became friends, and we've been friends ever since.'

Atreus lowered lush black lashes over his shimmering dark golden gaze. He had not taken to Ben, and the admission that she had once been in love with the other man simply underlined his reservations. But Atreus was proud of the fact that he had never experienced the urge to be possessive with his lovers. He met her strained violet-blue gaze and suddenly smiled, because he could read her like a book. She was pleased that he had invited her to lunch, but still nervous of being seen out in his company.

'We'll eat in the hotel suite,' Atreus murmured, closing a hand over hers to urge her across the depth of seat separating them.

'Atreus…' she gasped, in the aftermath of a

long, drugging kiss that left her feeling intoxicated. 'Throughout the history of the world there couldn't be two people less suited than us.'

'You have such old-fashioned ideas, but I like them,' Atreus growled, his mouth following a line down her neck to her throat that made her shiver violently, every nerve-ending screaming on high alert. 'Just as you like this—don't you?'

'Well…er…'

'Tell the truth,' he prompted lethally.

'It just feels indecent, and that's not who I am or what I'm like!' Lindy protested with the shattered incomprehension of a woman suddenly finding herself flat on the backseat of a limo in broad daylight.

'But the bottom line is that you like it, *glikia mou*,' Atreus replied with irrefutable logic. 'As for you not being like this, what would you know about who you really are when you waited so long to take a lover? Educating you promises to be a very exciting exercise.'

A lean hand sketched a provocative line

along the tautness of her inner thigh below her trousers and she honestly thought she might spontaneously combust from the level of heat and longing centred at the heart of her. Her lashes slid down. What had come over her? Where had all her common sense and caution gone? Into twenty-six years of clean living, low self-esteem and loneliness, a little voice answered. Not a bad life, but undeniably a life without any breathtaking highs.

'Do we have to eat first?' Atreus said huskily in an erotic growl.

Lindy tried and failed to swallow. Excitement was clawing at her, and no matter how hard she fought it she could already see how much influence he had over her and how much she was changing. If that was the effect he could have in twenty-four hours… But it wouldn't, couldn't, last long between them. It was a kind of madness, an attraction of opposites: sudden, startling and sexy, but surely destined to burn out fast. And when it was over she would be miserable….

Lindy looked up into his lean, dark beautiful face and decided that she could live with the prospect of that misery if it meant that she had him all to herself for a little while.

Four months later, Lindy and Atreus were still together almost every weekend.

By now Lindy was madly in love, and so happy she wakened with a smile on her face. But her mood was punctured suddenly one day by the sight of a photo in a gossip column. Atreus with another woman. It had been taken at a charity ball and the beautiful brunette was curved round Atreus like a second skin. Lindy felt quite sick looking at the photo, but she told herself that she would make no mention of the matter. She did not want to act possessively. The very idea of it hurt her pride, and she knew he would have a low tolerance threshold for such behaviour.

But after a couple of nights of disturbed sleep she realised she could not keep silent. They were lovers, and she needed the assurance that she was the only one in his life. When she dined with Atreus at Chantry House that weekend, Lindy planned to use subtlety to introduce the delicate subject of what he did when he was away from her during the week.

The graceful Georgian mansion had been restored to its former splendour in record time by builders and decorators working round the clock in shifts. Standing on the sidelines, Lindy had found that efficient restoration project highly educational. Atreus had not lowered his standards of excellence by so much as an inch, and the feat had been completed in a timeframe which most people had deemed impossible.

When no useful opening to the controversial topic occurred during their meal Lindy became increasingly restless and distracted.

'What's the matter with you?' Atreus asked as they vacated the dining table.

Feeling like a total coward for having failed to raise the subject, Lindy glanced at him uneasily. 'What do you mean?'

'You're very quiet, *mali mou*. It's not like you.'

'There was a photo of you with another woman in a gossip column this week.' In spite of her intention to make a light, non-accusatory enquiry when it came to the point, Lindy simply blurted out the facts and then cringed at her lack of skill.

Even though he knew exactly who, when and where, and even which newspaper, Atreus was too practised at keeping his own counsel with women to admit the fact. 'Was there?'

'You attended a charity ball with her.' Taut with tension and anxiety now, Lindy spun round in the drawing room, where drinks were being served and stared at him with strained eyes. 'Who was she?'

'A friend... I have many,' Atreus responded smoothly.

Painful colour lit Lindy's cheeks. 'You don't think I have any right to ask, do you? But I don't expect to be one of a crowd when I'm sleeping with you,' she shared, in an awkward rush of words.

The conscience that rarely troubled Atreus stung him in the face of that honest admission. Although he had found it safest and easiest never to define the boundaries of relationships, or make promises he might not wish to keep, her naive candour on the issue and her obvious concern pierced his emotional armour.

'Lindy—'

'Just tell me the truth. I have to know. To be honest, I've hardly slept a wink since I saw that photo,' she confessed unevenly.

Atreus reached for her hand and used it to propel her under his arm, ignoring her taut, stiff posture. 'I thought you would be more sensible,' he reproved. 'I only ever have one lover at a time, but I have many female acquaintances who act as my companions at various charitable and stuffy social engagements.'

Her heart still beating very fast with the apprehension that had built up in her since first seeing that photo, Lindy breathed easily again. She felt quite light-headed with relief. *I only ever have one lover at a time.* That was the one thing she had needed to hear. It shook her to appreciate that she had set no parameters at all in their relationship. Then she had fallen into it and then fallen crazily in love so fast she had never thought about rules. In any case Atreus, she recognised ruefully, was the sort of guy who would probably want to break a rule as soon as anyone was foolish enough to try and impose one on him.

In the early hours, she lay awake while he slept. Her body was heavy with tiredness, languor and sensual satisfaction. Her heart was light with love and contentment. But her mind was still racing over the conversation they had had after dinner. Although his response had given her peace of mind, she was convinced she had lost stature in his eyes by betraying her desperate need for reassurance. She could not escape the suspicion that she had ended up looking weak and insecure, which was not an impression that she wanted to give for Atreus was much more intrigued by strong, confident women. And that was what she was now,

Lindy consoled herself. Strong and confident and not in need of reassurance. It was not a slip she would make a second time.

Over a year after Lindy reached that decision, Ben Halliwell made one of his increasingly frequent unannounced visits to The Lodge. Having abandoned the pot pourri she had been bagging in the cellar, Lindy invited him in for coffee. He polished off two homemade cheese scones before coming to the point.

'If you really want to know where you stand with Atreus Dionides, you need to look at this.' Ben settled a page torn from a magazine down on the table in front of Lindy.

Caught unawares, Lindy stared and saw an image that shot the equivalent of a flaming arrow of pain right through her heart. Her skin broke out in perspiration and nausea made her tummy lurch. Once again it was a photograph of Atreus with another woman on his arm: a very beautiful blonde with jewels at her throat and a fancy evening gown. With a clumsy hand Lindy thrust the picture back at Ben in rejection, a look of reproof in her steady gaze. After all, it was not the first time she had seen such a photo, and she reckoned that it would not be the last. But she was annoyed with Ben, who never missed an opportunity to criticise Atreus or to try and show him in a bad light.

'Atreus was attending a charity benefit for a children's hospice on Monday night,' Lindy explained. 'That woman is probably one of the organisers.'

'Stop telling yourself whoppers and making excuses for him!' Ben's exasperation was unconcealed. 'Carrie Hetherington is a wealthy, well-connected socialite, and he's obviously not ashamed to be seen out in public with her—'

'Atreus is not ashamed of me, either,' Lindy argued vehemently. 'You're not being fair to him. I was the one who asked him to be discreet about our relationship, not the other way round. I didn't want to be seen out and about with him...I didn't want people gossiping about us, and I would die if my photo appeared in the newspapers!'

Ben groaned out loud. 'How can you still be so naive? He's not being discreet, Lindy. He's made you a dirty little secret in his life.'

Lindy rammed her hands down on the table surface and plunged upright. 'That's a horrible thing to say!'

Momentarily, Lindy saw stars as a bout of dizziness engulfed her. Assuming she had stood up too quickly, she breathed in slow and deep until the feeling of being light-headed receded.

'Whether you like it or not, it's the truth,' Ben continued, without even noticing how pale she had become. 'You're his mistress, not his girlfriend, and he only ever sees you at weekends, when he's down here. He never takes you out.'

'I'm not his mistress!' Lindy hissed back at Ben in passionate rejection of that label.

'But you're not a size zero hottie from his world, either. So exactly where do you fit in?'

Wounded by Ben's cutting reference, Lindy

studied him with pained eyes. 'Why are we even having this conversation? Why are you always attacking Atreus?'

'We've been friends for years and Atreus has spent the last eighteen months messing you around. It's a dead-end affair. The way he treats you he might as well be a married man, and you might as well be his bit on the side.'

'Atreus treats me very well!' Lindy argued, dropping back down into her chair.

'He's a billionaire. He can afford to be generous.'

'I'm not talking about money,' she said with distaste. 'You don't understand what we have.'

'I think you're the one who doesn't understand. You fell in love with him and started living in a cosy little dream world. You seem to have suspended every critical faculty you ever had. I'm only trying to wake you up. You're wasting your time with Dionides. He's not going to give you what you want,' Ben completed with ringing conviction.

'You don't know what I want.'

'Don't I?' Ben gave her an ironic look. 'This life is all wrong for you. You want marriage and security, but you've settled for an affair that you persist in viewing as the height of romance. Answer me one question. If you're so happy with Atreus, why have you still not got around to introducing him to Elinor and Alissa?'

'Elinor and Alissa aren't in the UK very often,' Lindy said defensively. One of whom lived in the Middle East and the other also spent a fair amount of time abroad.

'Do they even know that Dionides exists?'

Lindy reddened, because he had come closer to the truth than she was prepared to admit with that question. Only a few weeks had passed since she had finally phoned Elinor and Alissa to tell them about Atreus. 'Yes, of course they do, but I don't want to talk about this any more. I get very annoyed when you criticise Atreus, and I can't possibly discuss my relationship with him with you.'

'Just think over what I've said,' Ben urged. 'Or ask Dionides where your relationship is going. I guarantee that you won't like the response he gives you.'

To change the subject, Lindy asked him about his recent advancement at work. No topic could have been closer to Ben's heart. Her tension began to evaporate, but a leaden, hollow feeling still sat in her stomach.

'I have my boss's wedding to attend two weeks from now,' Ben informed her when he was on the brink of leaving. 'I thought of you immediately because it's being held at Headby Hall, which is only a few miles from here. I know it's short notice, but will you come with me as my partner?'

Lindy looked at him in surprise. 'I don't know. I—'

'Please,' Ben sighed. 'I would look sad, turning up on my own.'

Lindy laughed at the image of Ben looking sad, while dimly wondering why his once busy love-life had slowed down so much of late. He no longer had a new woman in his life every few weeks and, with more time on his hands, she had seen a great deal more of him in recent months. 'All right, give me the date and I'll mark it on my calendar.'

'Will it cause trouble between you and Atreus?' Ben asked with a hint of mockery.

'Of course it won't cause trouble.' Her chin tilted. 'Atreus doesn't question what I do.'

Brave words, Lindy acknowledged after Ben's departure. In truth she rarely did anything at weekends that would disrupt her time with Atreus, and he and Ben had not hit it off at their one and only meeting. Her mood had been buoyant before Ben's arrival, because it was a Friday and she would be with Atreus again in just a few hours. But Ben's comments had hit home hard. He had spoilt her day by making her question her relationship with Atreus.

As a rule Lindy lived from weekend to weekend, and nothing in between really mattered. It was just time to be got through before she saw Atreus again. Until Ben had cruelly thrust that wretched photo beneath her nose she had managed to pretty much ignore the reality that Atreus inhabited another world entirely when he was away from her. Was that because she had stopped buying newspapers and magazines after seeing Atreus in print with another female companion?

That was a tough question, and one that Lindy couldn't answer. Atreus had long since explained the reality that those acquaintances were of a social rather than intimate nature. The more she got to know Atreus the more she had grown to trust him, and the affair that she had once assumed would swiftly burn out had lasted and deepened.

In fact Lindy had lived on a high of happiness for almost eighteen months. Atreus phoned her almost every day. And he genuinely cared about her. He did. He might not show it in an emotional manner, for he was not a man given to issuing constant compliments or verbal reassurances, but he certainly demonstrated his concern in other ways. Hadn't he flown back from Greece when he'd learned that she was in hospital because she'd been knocked off her bike by a car? Hadn't she wakened to find him seated by her bed in the middle of the night? Hadn't she come home to find a brand-new hatchback car waiting to glide into the parking space being cut out of the lawn that bounded the drive for her benefit?

They had had their first real argument over that car. She had refused to accept it, and he had ranted about how dangerous the bike was, until the dissension between them had reached such a peak that she'd given way out of a genuine fear of losing him. The only other bone of contention between them was his ongoing refusal to accept rent from her as one of his tenants.

'How do you expect me to accept your money?' Atreus had demanded angrily. 'You work long hours to make a living. Do you think I don't know that? Why should you pay rent to me when I have more money than I could spend in one lifetime?'

That debate was still continuing in the background, for while Lindy doggedly continued to ensure that the rent was paid every month, Atreus continued to have the money returned to her bank account. When she stopped to wonder what the estate manager must think of the whole stupid business, she just cringed. All too many people were well aware of her involvement with the owner of the Chantry estate. It had been naive of her to imagine it could be otherwise. She had even run into the vicar of her church one afternoon at Chantry House. Atreus had innumerable staff as well. People knew, but minded their own business; it had taken Ben to confront her head-on. But what right had he to talk? Ben who, as far as she knew, had never once had a serious relationship with a woman.

Around six that evening Lindy came down the stairs with her weekend bag and her dogs. She was wearing a well-cut grey pencil skirt with a fine purple sweater, and black patent shoes with high heels. Since she had met Atreus she had gradually transformed her wardrobe and her appearance. Newly found confidence in her body had persuaded her to experiment with more figure-flattering garments. Her old shapeless skirts and loose sweaters had gone to the church jumble sale. Her hair had been styled from a haphazard mop into a sleek bouncy mane that framed her face, and she had rediscovered make-up.

But if Atreus had noticed a single change while she polished up her image he hadn't mentioned it, Lindy acknowledged wryly. Nor had her improved looks given him the urge to take her out and show her off. Why was she so contrary, though? In spite of her having once told him that she didn't want to be seen out in public with him, she now craved such an invitation. But she was not about to ask Atreus any stupid questions about the future. She was secure and happy as she was...

Twenty minutes later the limo drew up outside and Lindy, with her dogs at her heels, climbed in. The luxury vehicle whisked them up to the big house. The chauffeur opened the door and sidestepped the dogs to greet her. Phoebe Carstairs only worked weekdays. Every weekend a French chef and several Greek menservants came down in advance of Atreus's arrival and took charge of the household to ensure the assiduous level of service and attention to detail that the tycoon expected from his staff. There was lightness in Lindy's step and a bubbling anticipation inside her. Following the path of Dmitri's helpful hand, she headed straight for the library, which Atreus used as an office…

CHAPTER FOUR

A STUNNING vision of masculine style in a charcoal-grey business suit flawlessly tailored to his tall, well-built frame, Atreus was poised by the library's elegant windows while he talked on the phone. For a split second Lindy paused to refresh her eyes with the sight of him and revel in the pleasure of seeing him again. He swung round, his lean, breathtakingly handsome features briefly shedding their often sombre aspect with a sudden flashing smile. Samson and Sausage squeezed past Lindy to race across the room and hurl themselves at him. Knowing that that energetic welcome would go down like a lead balloon while he was on the phone, Lindy threw herself in the dogs' path and acted as a barrier between her lover and her pets.

Atreus closed a steadying arm round her as the impact of the animals against the back of her legs almost unbalanced her. The glow of warmth in her eyes captivated him. He liked the way she never hid anything from him, never tried to play it cool. He found her as straightforward as he found others of her sex artificial. As the evocative scent of her hair and her skin made his nostrils flare, he was instantly aware of the erotic pulse at his groin. He lowered his head to press his skilful mouth hotly to a tender spot just below her ear, a move he had long since learned drove her wild. With a sensual moan of surrender, Lindy quivered with the delicious awakening that was hurtling like liquid fire to her every pulse-point and nerve-ending. Atreus said something rather abrupt into his phone, set it down, and hauled her to him with impatient hands to kiss her breathless.

'A weekend isn't enough for me when it's followed by five days of celibacy,' he growled when he finally let her breathe again.

Lindy was thrilled by that admission. 'I suppose I could come up to London occasionally,' she began, eager to gain an entrance into that other part of his world which had so far been closed to her.

His jawline clenched. 'I like things the way they are. I'm free to concentrate on business during the week. We both have plenty of space.'

Her eyes dimmed. She didn't want that space, had never wanted that space, and only put up with his frequent unavailability in silence because it seemed to be what he expected from her. That belated admission shook her. Just when had she started fitting in with his wishes and ignoring her own? But what woman wanted her lover to see her as clingy? she asked herself defensively. Atreus might be her only source of experience, but she knew that a needy, demanding woman could make a man feel trapped.

Cursing the insecurity that Ben's outspoken criticism had roused in her, Lindy blanked out her anxious thoughts and rested back in the seemingly secure circle of Atreus's arms.

She loved him so much, and she had a whole weekend to luxuriate in. Was she about to let her lack of confidence spoil what they shared? She hadn't intended to fall for him—had thought intelligence would help her to hold back and protect herself from getting too attached to a man who was unlikely to stay with her. But there had been no protection from his innate charisma and high-voltage sexuality, or the clever brain that consistently intrigued and entertained her. She sank deeper and deeper into love every time she saw him. By the end of the first three months of their affair she had been a totally lost cause.

Atreus was suspicious of her sudden suggestion that she see him in London during the week. Where had that unfortunate idea come from? Had the one-time love of her life been muckraking again? Atreus wondered grimly, for he was already aware that Lindy's alleged friend had visited her that afternoon. Ben Halliwell was a thorn in Atreus's side, playing a waiting game and always ready to make trouble. Lindy was so impressionable, Atreus reflected ruefully, keeping her close while he smoothed a soothing hand down over her taut spine, recognising her mood of disquiet with growing annoyance. Perhaps it was time that he had a word with Halliwell and warned him off. Lindy, who thought the best of everyone and the least of herself, would never do it for him. Evidently it had not yet occurred to her that her old friend now wanted what he had so carelessly rejected at university, and Atreus was in no hurry to point out Ben's change of heart.

'I missed you,' she confided, only to regret the revealing admission as soon as the words left her lips.

His arms tightened round her. 'The week went very slowly,' he conceded, letting his mouth graze over hers and then return to part her lips with a sudden hungry urgency that sent the blood hurtling in a mad race through her veins. Her knees went weak, the tug of craving in her pelvis almost more than she could bear in silence. It had not taken him long to teach her that desire could be a cruel task-master, for while her brain teemed with troubled thoughts and fears, her body was only capable of craving the urgency of his. Lindy closed her eyes tight in frustration, fighting to restrain the intensity of her longing, hating the knowledge that she only ever felt really secure in bed with him. That was when she felt most needed and valued, and what did that say about their relationship?

'What's wrong?' Atreus murmured.

Lindy cursed his sixth sense where she was concerned, his unexpected ability to pick up on what she was feeling. 'Nothing.'

Although he was unimpressed by that obvious falsehood, Atreus was too hot for her to hold back. He lifted her up to him and plundered her mouth with a need and intensity that made her head spin and her arms wrap round his neck. 'Dinner will be late tonight,' he told her thickly.

It took only a clipped word from Atreus to restrain the dogs from following them upstairs.

Her heart was pounding when he lowered her down in the bedroom. Unzipped, her skirt shimmied down over her hips. Her sweater was tossed aside. With an earthy, masculine sound of satisfaction, Atreus appraised the succulent swell of her creamy breasts within her bra and lifted her onto the bed, pulling off her shoes in the process.

'By Friday lunchtime you are all I can think about,' he said huskily, long fingers briefly framing her face as he claimed another kiss and unclipped the bra to gain full access to her luscious curves.

'I thought we were going to talk,' Lindy framed breathlessly, fighting the erotic languor overcoming her and the paralysis of intelligent thought.

Having already shed his jacket and tie, and unbuttoned his shirt, Atreus sank down on the bed beside her with a groan of reluctant amusement. 'The state you've got me in, I'm not fit to talk, *mali mou.*'

Her fingers splaying across the bronzed hair-roughened contours of his superb torso, Lindy could not even think about what it was that she had believed she'd wanted to talk about as other, more basic promptings took charge of her. The burning and dampness gathering between her thighs ignited an almost unbearable yearning. His lips closed round a distended pink nipple while he skimmed off her panties. The very first touch of his mouth on her torturously tender flesh made her spine swoop off the mattress in a responsive arch. Her heart thundered and her legs trembled when he teased the sensitive bud below her mound. Very quickly she reached a saturation point of arousal, when waiting became an intolerable torment, and a pleading moan of protest parted her lips.

'You couldn't possibly want me yet as much as I want you, *glikia mou*,' Atreus countered with fierce conviction, strong hands anchoring to her hips to pull her under him.

But as her body braced for his possession he fell back from her with a stifled curse and reached for the protection he had almost forgotten 'We don't want any mistakes in the contraception department,' he told her, with a grim edge to his rich dark drawl. 'That would wreck everything.'

Even as he drove into her wildly receptive body that edge in his voice lingered in her memory and chilled her. She suppressed her disquiet and told herself he was only being sensible. He sank his hands below her hips and plunged deeper into her. The delirious pleasure his lovemaking always gave her had taken on an unfamiliar driven urgency. Excitement was cascading through her in a dazzling storm of white-hot sparks. He ground into her and she gasped, what remained of her control melted by the flames of excitement. His wildness thrilled her and the ecstatic climax she reached took her body's capacity for enjoyment to new heights. Even as the exquisite waves of erotic bliss consumed her, she was conscious that she was crying—and shocked by the fact.

'I must have been good, *glikia mou,*' Atreus breathed with irrepressible satisfaction, holding her locked in his arms and kissing her before falling still to stare down into her wide shaken eyes. 'We share the most unbelievable chemistry. No other woman has ever given me so much pleasure in bed.'

Lindy cherished the rare compliment that made her feel more important than any of her more glamorous predecessors, but her mind was still working back over what he had said only minutes earlier.

'Why did you say a mistake with contraception would wreck everything?'

Atreus tensed. 'Because it's the truth. I don't want a child with you.'

Inside herself, where he couldn't see, Lindy, who loved children and who had dreamt in whimsical moments of having his baby, recoiled from that cruel candour. Her dreams were suffering an axe attack. 'Don't you like children?' she asked.

An alarm bell was by now ringing in Atreus's

handsome dark head, and his ebony brows drew together in a frown. She had never admitted it, but he knew how much she liked babies. Her friends sent her photos of their children and she gushed over them. Months ago he had reached the conclusion that the homeless dogs and cats she doted on were most probably substitutes for the babies she would one day have.

'A couple of paternity battles took the edge off any desire I might have to reproduce,' Atreus confided, opting for the truth.

'Paternity battles?' Lindy parroted in dismay. 'Are you saying that you already have a child?'

'None that I know of—a reality that some women have in the past chosen to regard as a challenge.'

Lindy collided with hard dark eyes and recognised that this reality still had the power to rouse his anger. 'In what way…a challenge?'

'A rich man is a lucrative target in the paternity stakes,' he extended with rich cynicism.

'Thankfully, DNA tests proved that I was not the father of either child. But if I hadn't been able to prove that I would have been made financially responsible for those women and their offspring for many years to come.'

'Naturally you wouldn't want a child in those circumstances,' Lindy remarked with understanding.

'I will only want a child when I'm married.'

That declaration hung there like a second slap in the face; having already told her that he didn't want a child with her, or until he was married, he was effectively letting her know that she was not in the running as a potential wife. Had she thought she might be? Lindy eased away from him with the stealth of a mouse hoping to escape a cat ready to pounce. All of a sudden, lying in Atreus's arms no longer felt like a safe and proper harbour.

'And what sort of woman are you planning to marry?' she heard herself enquire. Having gone so far, she thought she might as well fully satisfy her curiosity.

Atreus skimmed a glance at her pale, pinched profile. 'I don't think we should stray any deeper into this conversation.'

'Atreus, it's clear that you've already thought in depth about your future and planned it all out,' Lindy pointed out in a tight, stretched tone he had never heard from her lips before. 'I think it's a reasonable question for me to ask after the length of time we've been together.'

Annoyed with her for opening the subject in the first place, and disregarding his every attempt to head her off at the pass, Atreus rested simmering golden eyes on her. 'I'll marry a wealthy woman from a background similar to my own.'

Until that deeply wounding moment Lindy had not appreciated just how far her dreams had gone. Nor had she grasped how painful it might be to realise that she had never had and could never have a chance of becoming a contender in the bridal stakes. She had neither wealth nor background to impress him with, and as such could never be anything other than a casual lover on his terms. In an abrupt movement, she snaked out of bed and began to get dressed in haste.

Ben's confident assurance that she wouldn't like the answer she got from Atreus was already reverberating like a death knell in her ears. Atreus didn't love her. Feeling as he did, how could he possibly care for her in any way? He didn't even see her as being in any way special. That she was poor, industrious and the child of working class uneducated parents would always hang on her like a badge of shame in his eyes.

'Lindy…what's going on here?' Atreus demanded in growing exasperation.

'Nothing's going on,' she fielded flatly. 'But I do I think that you should have been more frank with me months ago. I didn't realise that I was in a dead-end affair.'

'What's dead-end about it?' Atreus raked back at her with splintering impatience. 'It's not as though I'm planning to get married any time soon!'

'You're such a snob, too!' Lindy delivered her judgement with scorn. 'I haven't got money or a fancy family tree, so you've never taken me seriously...'

Atreus was a vibrant male presence as he lounged back against the tossed pillows, his wide shoulders and bronzed torso providing a startling contrast with the plain white bedlinen. 'Why would I take you seriously?' he cut in lethally. 'We've had a good time together. Snobbery didn't come into it. In fact, it's more likely that the differences between us made our relationship more entertaining...'

'Well, I'm not finding it entertaining at this moment!' Lindy launched back at him, her lush mouth biting off that last word as she forced her lips shut again. She didn't trust herself. She could not be sure what words might come out of her mouth next, and she was fighting to retain a little dignity. Even so, she was devastated. The man she loved was talking down to her in the shallowest and most patronising way, telling her that they'd simply had a good time together when her feelings for him ran so much deeper and stronger. She had entertained him because her differences had provided him with a welcome diversion.

Atreus was stunned by Lindy's behaviour. From the outset of their affair he had enjoyed the fact that she didn't throw tantrums or suffer from petulant moods. She was calm, laid-back in temperament and sensible, not given to making unreasonable demands or staging arguments. She only revealed her passion between the sheets, where he found her eagerness for him insanely, brilliantly sexy.

He sprang out of bed, crossed the floor and lifted her off her feet without further ado.

'What the heck do you think you're doing?' Lindy demanded furiously.

'I'm taking you back to bed in the hope that you regain your senses, *glikia mou,*' Atreus imparted in an aggrieved tone.

'I'm not getting back into bed with you!' Lindy hissed, swatting away his hands and sliding straight back off the bed again. 'We're finished!'

CHAPTER FIVE

WITH a groan of disbelief, Atreus lay back against the tumbled pillows and studied Lindy's flushed and resolute face. 'I don't expect this kind of silly melodrama from you. You find out that we're not heading to the altar and that's it? It's all over? Doesn't that strike you as more than a little unreasonable?'

'No. Every word you've said makes it clear that you don't respect me or take me seriously in any way!' Lindy argued vehemently. 'I'm just someone you sleep with at weekends and never take out in public, and that's not enough for me.'

Atreus sat up in a sudden movement, anger stamped into every angular line of his hard, handsome face. 'It's been more than enough to keep you happy all this time—and do I have to remind you that you're the one who did not want to be seen out with me in public?'

'I'm your mistress!' Lindy condemned with a shudder of disgust. 'Aren't I?'

'That's an old-fashioned label and I'm not an old-fashioned guy,' Atreus fired back at her, seeing just how welcome candour would be at that precise instant.

'Can't you even admit that that's what I am?' Lindy shouted, her hands coiling into tight fists as she fought to get a grip on her self-control again.

Atreus lodged scorching golden eyes full of censure on her. 'Okay, you're my mistress.'

Eyes welling with stinging tears of shame and hatred, Lindy stared at him. She wanted to throw things and scream. She had wanted him to deny that she was his mistress, because that title struck her as the final humiliation.

'But that doesn't mean that you're not an important part of my life,' Atreus delivered with measured cool. 'You are important to me.'

'For sex, amusement…a woman to spice up

your country weekends who doesn't cause you any hassle,' she completed bitterly, her heart beating so fast and so loudly in her ears that she feared she might be on the edge of a panic attack, even though she had never had one before. But then she had never been in such pain. Pain that flailed her with self-loathing and anger and the most appalling sense of loss, for Atreus was so much a part of her life that she could barely muster the courage to even imagine a future without him.

His mistress—that was all she had ever been. All these months she had deceived herself with wishful thinking, imagining a deeper connection and assuming an equality that had never existed between them. A mistress: a woman who gave discreet sexual pleasure, stayed in the background of her lover's life and looked for nothing more than his approbation and financial support. No wonder he had been so determined to make her accept the car he had bought her, and no wonder he had refused her rent payments! After all, a mistress was supposed to be rewarded and even supported by her lover. That was the deal. Awkward questions such as she had just asked were not part of that deal.

'I do value you,' Atreus breathed in a raw undertone. 'I've never stayed with one woman as long as I have stayed with you.'

But Lindy had another angle entirely on the surprising longevity of their affair. Without challenging him with words of love, she had adored him, admired him and lived to please him. She had asked for nothing. Why would he have walked away from so convenient an arrangement? He said he valued her. But even when telling her that she was important to him he was careful to employ dispassionate words which promised nothing deep or lasting. The caution with which he spoke also warned her that Atreus Dionides had never had any doubts about her exact status and place in his life. A mistress was all she had ever been, and that she could ever have believed she might mean more to him now struck her as pathetic and laughable.

As the door thudded shut on her silent departure, Atreus ground out a roughened curse. What had got into Lindy? He would have sworn that he knew her inside out, but she was behaving like a stranger. Where had that temper come from? Where had those damnable questions come from? Out of the blue? Or was it Ben Halliwell he should be thanking for this denouement?

Atreus raked lean fingers through his tousled black hair, enraged by what had happened. He had been taken by surprise and he wasn't accustomed to that. How could she be so foolish? They were perfect together as they were. What was wrong with being his mistress? Hundreds of women would have killed to occupy her position. Labels and silly discussions about where they were going had never been necessary between them. She had never tried to subject him to such a conversation before. Why should she have done? He knew he made her happy and prided himself on that fact.

It cut both ways: she pleased him as well. When he needed to work she never voiced a word of objection; she would just go off to the animal sanctuary and put in a few hours there. Often he would end up looking for her. She was easy to be with, stubbornly independent, and well able to manage without him around. She had slotted into his schedule as though she had been tailor-made for the purpose.

But that did not empower her to make ridiculous demands and throw his generosity back in his teeth, and nor would he necessarily forgive her for those errors of judgement. Had she truly thought he might consider marrying her and having a family with her? Just as though he was some Joe Nobody instead of one of the richest men in the world, with a social pedigree in his Greek homeland that could be traced back several hundred years?

Was he so much a snob? When it came to matrimony, surely his family were entitled to have certain expectations of him? Hadn't his father's divorce, remarriage and subsequent loose lifestyle caused the Dionides family incessant grief and mortification? The family had had to pick up the pieces in the end: not his deluded father and his feckless mother, but his aunt and uncle, who had ultimately been landed with the task of raising him to adulthood. A responsible man did not marry out of his own order.

Atreus was as outraged with Lindy as he was frustrated by her departure. Just as quickly, however, he recalled his awareness at the outset of their arrangement that she had no idea of the rules he played by and was likely to be hurt. The logic was irrefutable: he should let her go now, close the book on their association.

Lindy had never known she had it in her to be as emotional as she was that night. Eyes dry, head held high, she had stalked back to the lodge on foot with her dogs, fury washing over her in heady bursts. But her anger with Atreus was no greater than her anger towards herself. Why on earth had she got involved with him?

She couldn't sleep, she tossed and turned, fell into a doze a couple of times and then, wakening, instinctively looked for him and went through the whole ghastly drowning sense of loss all over again. Samson and Sausage got up on the bed and lay beside her, pushing their heads under her hand, nudging her with their warm bodies in an effort to respond to her misery.

Atreus would never have let the dogs into the bedroom, never mind onto the bed, she reflected numbly, seeking some reason to celebrate their break-up. But still more tears leaked from her sore eyes. It had happened so fast that she had had no time to prepare, and now her whole world seemed empty and without structure. She was used to going horse riding first thing on Saturday mornings. Atreus had taught her to ride and had tipped her out of bed soon after dawn every Saturday without fail. When he wasn't involved in business he was relentlessly active, with buckets of surplus energy that required a physical outlet. Her face burned as she recalled how available she had always been—as hot for him as he was for her. Shifting uneasily in her bed, she frowned as a bout of nausea made her tummy lurch, and a moment later she flung herself out of bed and raced full tilt for the bathroom.

Lindy was almost never sick, and she wondered if her emotional distress had somehow affected her digestive system. As she freshened up she accidentally brushed her breast with her arm and winced at the painful tenderness of her flesh. She knew that some women experienced sore breasts during the latter half of their menstrual cycle but she'd had a light period only a few days ago. Her momentary tension faded. Obviously her hormones were out of sync and her body was going haywire, doing things it had never done before. But at least she had no grounds to suspect that she might have fallen pregnant, she told herself in urgent consolation.

Early on in her relationship with Atreus Lindy had begun taking contraceptive pills, but side effects had forced her to come off them again and give responsibility for protection back to Atreus. He had never taken the smallest risk with her which, bearing in mind his feelings on that issue, she reckoned painfully was fortunate. He would surely give an ex-mistress who had become pregnant with his child short shrift. It was not hard to assume that, put in such a situation, he would prefer a termination to an actual birth—an approach which would ensure that there was no permanent damage inflicted on his precious aristocratic family tree. She was very, very thankful that she was not being faced with that particular challenge.

That weekend Atreus returned to his London life early, and he did not visit the following week. Whenever he thought of his country home, he thought of Lindy, a fact which infuriated him since he had never considered himself to be remotely sensitive or even imaginative. Regardless, his memory threw up images of Chantry in which she always featured, and the merest hint of the scent of lavender made him grit his teeth.

He remembered the melting taste of her ginger fudge shortcake and wondered if he was entering his second childhood. He remembered how terrified she had been when he'd put her on a horse, although nothing would have made her admit the fact. He remembered that she never said a bad word about anyone, and that when he was late or curt she said nothing but simply looked disappointed in him, which somehow made him more punctual and more polite. He woke in the night, his body aching for her, and reached for her to find she wasn't there.

He had never had a problem with anger. He had never regretted breaking up with a woman. After all there was always another dozen queuing to fill the space in his bed. Every woman was replaceable; this was a mantra he had believed in from an early age. But even though he plunged straight back into socialising, he discovered that his tastes had changed.

He liked a woman to appreciate the value of a comfortable silence, one who ate without caring about calories, one who went out without fussing about her appearance, one who listened and responded with intelligence when he talked. And the less easy he found his search for a substitute the angrier and more frustrated he became.

The following Friday he was about to cancel his trip to Chantry again when it dawned on him that there was a solution to what ailed him.

He called his estate manager and freely admitted that he would like the tenant in The Lodge to relocate. He suggested that a substantial cash inducement be offered to bring about that desirable result. He travelled down to Chantry that afternoon.

He would not have looked in the direction of The Lodge at all, had he not noticed that Ben Halliwell's BMW was parked there. He frowned, still galled by the idea that this *agent provocateur* had contrived to escape unscathed from the trouble he had caused. Atreus opened the door of Chantry with a glum expression to discover the Georgian house horrendously quiet. There were no dogs to greet him with lolling pink tongues, shrill barks and frantic wagging tails…. Setting his even white teeth together, and reminding himself that he had never liked animals indoors, Atreus sat down to dine on the very best his French chef could offer. But the selection didn't include any ginger fudge shortcake.

That same afternoon, Lindy was grateful for the diversion of the evening wedding party she was to attend with Ben, although she was fairly sure that she wouldn't be eating anything at the supper. The stomach upset she had first suffered a couple of weeks earlier had since come back to haunt her on several occasions. Evidently she had caught a virus, and her body was finding it hard to shake it off. As such illnesses always ran their course, she saw no point in consulting her doctor. She'd put fresh linen on her own bed for Ben, having decided that it would be cruel to put someone as tall as him on a sofa for the night. She had had her hair done and had bought a misty-blue dress for the occasion. Ben was good company and she would enjoy herself.

Lindy was determined to cast off the awful sense of abandonment she had suffered in recent weeks. It was as if she and Atreus had never been together at all. No man had ever been more easily got rid of; he had not even tried to change her mind, which suggested that she had never been the slightest bit important to him. In time she would stop missing him, thinking about him all the time, crying herself to sleep. Some day, she told herself fiercely, she would be capable of saying, *Atreus...who?* and meaning it.

Ben could not conceal his satisfaction at having been right about Atreus when Lindy told him that the affair was over. Assuring her that time healed everything, and that she was far better off without her Greek lover, Ben promptly forgot the matter again while he got on with the important matter of socialising with the well-connected guests present at the wedding supper. Lindy longed for the solace of her female friends, Elinor and Alissa, believing that only another woman would understand what she was going through. She planned to phone them and tell them what was happening very soon.

Resolute in his goal of getting through the weekend in much the same way as he had always done, Atreus went out riding the following morning. From a distance of a hundred yards as he rode back across the park he saw Ben Halliwell's car, still parked in the exact same position as it had been the evening before. Halliwell had spent the night. With Lindy.

A thunderbolt of primeval rage roared through Atreus's powerful frame like a sudden all-encompassing storm. It was so potent that as he dug his knees into the stallion to head for The Lodge he was not conscious of any thought at all. Every atom of his anger and frustration had found a fitting focus at last.

Lindy had slept badly on the lumpy sofa. When the doorbell sounded the dogs went bonkers, barking. She rolled off the sofa, ignoring her feeling of nausea, and was putting on her cotton wrap when Ben shouted downstairs. 'Who the heck is that at this hour?'

'Haven't a clue,' she called back.

'It might be for me. Geoffrey Stillwood did say something about inviting me out for a day's hunting,' Ben reminded her. 'Not something I've tried before, but I should show willing if the invite is issued by my boss's father-in-law!'

Lindy's nose wrinkled at the thought of deer being killed for sport. It had been a challenge for her to keep her views to herself while she'd listened to that conversation the night before. Tightening the sash of her wrap, she opened the front door. Her eyes opened very wide at the sight of Dino, Atreus's black stallion, cropping the lawn. Atreus, sheathed in tight jodhpurs, polished boots and a black jerkin, was on her doorstep, and even his worst enemy would have been forced to admit that he looked drop-dead gorgeous in that get-up.

As Samson and Sausage charged out and careered round Atreus's feet in rapturous doggy welcome, stunning dark golden eyes lanced into her. 'It didn't take you very long to take another man into your bed,' Atreus condemned with seething scorn.

'I'll take care of this,' Ben announced from behind Lindy, pushing her to one side to gain the space to step out. Unshaven, and in jeans, boots and a sweater, it was obvious he had got up in a hurry.

'Do you think you can?' Atreus sent him a contemptuous look of challenge. 'I'm not in the habit of fighting over loose women.'

'There's not going to be any fighting,' Lindy assured him indignantly, only to fall silent, her jaw dropping and her lips framing a silent 'oh' of shock and horror when Ben took a swing at Atreus and struck him on the chin.

'Don't talk about Lindy like that!' Ben slung at the tall Greek, full blast.

'How unexpected—a City trader who can put his money where his mouth is!' With that sardonic quip, Atreus punched Ben so hard that the blond man hit the ground like a fallen tree.

Thirty seconds later, as a groaning Ben began clambering shakily upright for another bout, Lindy stepped between the two men and voiced outraged words of reproof. 'No! Stop it right now!'

'Stay out of this,' Atreus urged, powerful arms closing round Lindy from behind to lift her bodily out of his path and set her out of harm's way.

'Don't you dare tell me to stay out of it!' Lindy raked back furiously at him, just as the sound of a perky mobile phone ring-tone cut through the tense atmosphere.

Atreus strode back to attack just as Ben dug out his phone and answered it, raising a hand palm first to Atreus in a ludicrous gesture that urged his Greek opponent to give him a moment's breathing space.

'Geoff? Hello, Geoff… No, of course it's not too early for me,' Ben was saying in a smarmy tone while checking his watch. 'I would love to… When? Right, I'll be there as soon as I can.'

Wearing a newly purposeful expression, Ben swung round to Lindy in haste. 'Where's the nearest country clothing shop?'

Somewhat taken aback by that sudden request, Lindy obliged with the information. Ben then raced back indoors to collect his stuff, all desire to continue his fight with Atreus in her defence evidently forgotten in his excitement at being invited out on a shoot by a member of the local gentry.

Atreus interpreted the expression of blank disbelief on Lindy's face. 'Financial traders have a reputation for being cold-blooded,' he remarked. 'No Greek male would ever stop to take a phone call in the middle of a fight.'

'If that's the best you can say for yourself it's

not a lot!' Lindy fired back, unimpressed. 'How dare you come here and suggest that I sleep around?'

Atreus lifted a broad shoulder in a slow mocking shrug, an ebony brow lifting. 'I'm not cold-blooded. I didn't think you'd get over me so quickly.'

Taken aback by the cruel comment that went too close to the bone for comfort, Lindy reddened but stayed silent on the score that she no longer owed him any explanations. She watched him take the lead rope hanging from the iron ring at the corner of the house and approach the black stallion. 'What on earth are you doing?' she asked.

'What do you think?'

Lindy didn't know what to say, because sensitivity made her shrink from mentioning past intimacies. On several occasions when they had been out riding they had tied up the horses outside The Lodge and fallen laughing and breathless into her bed below the eaves, hungry to sate the desire that rarely left them.

She did not want to recall those painfully sweet memories which had evidently meant so much more to her than to him.

Ben brushed by her with a muffled apology and a hasty promise to ring during the following week. It was as if his angry conflict with Atreus had never happened. She wondered if Atreus could really believe that she had slept with Ben. Did that mean that he had never trusted her friendship with the other man? Or was Atreus simply being insulting because she had dumped him?

When Atreus was sure that he had tethered Dino securely, he strolled back to Lindy, six foot three inches of devastatingly handsome masculinity. Involuntarily, she found herself staring, helplessly feasting her starved eyes on him. Clad in riding gear, Atreus was every woman's fantasy. In close-fitting breeches and boots, he possessed a male beauty and sleek grace of movement that knocked her sideways. Desire infiltrated Lindy in a heady surge, and her mouth ran dry and her knees went wobbly.

'Why are you tying up Dino?'

Hot golden eyes slammed into hers and she felt the burn of that sexual smoulder low in her pelvis. He meshed one hand into her tumbled brown mane, tipping her head back so that his mouth could come down hard on hers. As he backed her indoors her senses swam and her heartbeat raced. Shock and satisfaction tore her composure apart. 'We can't…'

Atreus kicked the front door shut behind him and pressed her back against the panelled wall of the hall. 'Tell me no,' he challenged.

But the sensual taste of him was on her lips again, and like a shameful addict she could not resist her craving. Just one kiss, she told herself, bargaining with her conscience. Just one more kiss, she thought a split second later, while he crushed her against the wall and acquainted her with every muscular line of his lean, powerful body. He plundered her soft mouth, nibbling, stroking and delving into the sensitive interior until he had sent her temperature rocketing to a crazy height.

She rejoiced in the hard muscular heat of him, all logic overpowered by his passionate urgency and the rigid swell of his erection against her.

Lean hands glided upward, pushing her wrap and nightdress out of his path even while she tensed and trembled. A tight knot of desire had formed inside her and she tried to fight it—even when a little voice in her head dared to whisper that Atreus had seemed to be jealous of Ben. Could he have missed her so much that he was now trying to get her back? In the state she was in, giving credence to such thoughts was fatal.

Atreus nudged her legs apart to probe the slick honeyed folds between her thighs. Beneath his ministrations she moaned and leant back against the wall for support. Once he had centred his attentions on the tender swollen bud below the soft curls on her mound tingling ripples of seductive delight controlled her, and no thought, no word or warning could have returned her to solid earth again. She stretched up on tiptoes to savour the driving hunger of his sensual mouth again.

Atreus closed both arms round her and swept her off her feet. Sexual need had never driven him with such ferocity. He felt like a runaway train, hurtling down a mountain, and it was an amazingly exhilarating experience. He carried her up the stairs into the bedroom and tumbled her down on the rumpled bedding, pushing up the wrap and the nightdress so that he could savour her voluptuous curves to the full.

A soundless sigh of appreciation escaped him as his lustful gaze locked to the glorious bounty of her breasts. He came down on the bed to suckle the tantalisingly distended pink nipples and mould the soft creamy fullness of her flesh with deep satisfaction. Preoccupied as he was with those distractions, it took effort for him to free a hand and withdraw a condom from his pocket, to unsnap his jodhpurs, wrenching down the zip with unhidden impatience.

Lindy was on a high of trembling expectation. Two of the things she most loved about

Atreus were his unpredictability and his un-
ashamed passion for her body. She saw his
urgency as a compliment which only matched
her own for him. Before he could don protection she pushed herself up and pleasured his
straining sex with her tongue.

'No,' he ground out in a voice of aching
gratification. 'You'll make me come, *mali mou.*'

Empowered by the realisation that he was
trembling with eagerness, Lindy fell back
again. He gripped her hips and arched her
back, sinking with a driven groan into her lush
opening in a long, deep thrust. A frenzy of excitement gripped her as he lifted her up to
receive his every stroke. The surge and ebb of
his body into hers was primal and pagan, and
she writhed in abandonment beneath that
fierce onslaught of pleasure and possession.
Nothing had ever been wilder or more satisfy-
ing, and the end came for them both in an
intense climax that made his magnificent
length shudder over her.

Frantic confusion assailed Lindy in the aftermath of their lovemaking, for she had no script to follow and no idea what she had been thinking of when she'd allowed things to go so far. Her overwhelming hunger for him had been satisfied but at what cost? she wondered in painful mortification.

Atreus emerged from the same experience shell-shocked. He was unnerved by the acknowledgement that he had been out of control for the first time in his life. His mood was not improved when his attention fell on the man's black bow tie lying on the carpet by the bed. Halliwell's tie…obviously. Distaste filled Atreus, and his reaction was instantaneous. He pulled away from Lindy and sprang off the bed to stride into the bathroom next door.

In the silence, Lindy tugged down her disarranged clothing and shuddered at what she had allowed to happen. He had neither held her nor kissed her afterwards; everything had changed between them; everything was different. She slid off the bed on nerveless legs, her body still quivering from the rampant impact of his and the excruciatingly tender state of it in the aftermath of his devouring passion. Like a woman running from the scene of a crime, she sped downstairs.

Atreus splashed his face and dried it. He was seething with anger and a daunting sense of bewilderment. He had not wanted sex since he'd left her. But he never, ever went back to a woman. When it was over, it was over. He had always walked away from relationships before they could reach the messy stage, but what had just occurred had been messy to say the very least. Brilliant, fantastic sex, he conceded bitterly, but inappropriate—particularly when she had wasted no time in inviting another man into her bed.

He had wanted Lindy again only because she was familiar, he decided grimly. But since when had he found the familiar so appealing? So sexually irresistible? Had he grown past the age where he wanted a constant parade of variety in the bedroom? Was he now ready for a more settled lifestyle? Perhaps it was time for him to begin looking out for a wife rather than another lover. That bold step forward in thought, away from Lindy and on to a more traditional horizon, pleased Atreus and steadied his resolve.

'I'm sorry,' Atreus breathed coldly, when he found Lindy waiting for him in the living room.

'I'm not sure I understand what you're apologising for,' Lindy admitted stiltedly, frantically avoiding direct eye contact. She sensed his detachment and it chilled her that he could switch off again so easily.

'What we had is over and done with,' Atreus declared without hesitation. 'I shouldn't be here when I don't want you back.'

Lindy marvelled that she managed to continue breathing through the savage sense of rejection that that blunt declaration had dealt her. He had dragged her off to bed and made passionate love to her but it had meant absolutely nothing to him. Indeed, his hostile attitude made it clear that he very much regretted their renewed intimacy.

'You know...' Lindy began hesitantly, de-

spising herself in advance for the plea of in-
nocence she was about to make without any
encouragement from him. 'I didn't sleep with
Ben. I slept down here on the sofa.'

Against his own volition Atreus directed
grim dark eyes at the sofa and the bedding still
lying on it in an untidy heap. He looked away
again, refusing to dwell on what she had said,
refusing the suggestion that the information
could have any power to influence him. 'It
doesn't matter. You're not my business any
more,' he said drily. 'I crossed boundaries I
had no right to cross today. It won't happen
again.'

Watching Atreus leave, Lindy felt as if
someone was squeezing her heart dry of blood.
She couldn't breathe for the pain of it. She
watched him ride off from the window and
then drew back to cover her tear-wet face with
trembling hands. She felt sick again, and she
wanted to bang her head against the wall to
hurt herself—because she felt that she
deserved to be punished for the way she had

let herself down. How could she have been so foolish as to go to bed with him again? Particularly after he had suggested she was a loose woman? Where was her self-respect? She and Atreus had never been on a level playing field. It seemed that his convenient affair had been her heartbreak…

CHAPTER SIX

FORTY-EIGHT hours later, Lindy was doggedly engaged in packing orders for her customers, in preparation for heading off to the post office, when the doorbell rang. She had to sign for the envelope the postman gave her, and she tore it open with a frown.

It was a notice to quit The Lodge for non-payment of rent, and it requested that she move out within two months. Lindy's eyes were wide with disbelief. In recent months she had received a couple of letters pointing out that she owed the Chantry estate rent arrears. When the second letter had arrived she had gone to the estate office in person, to point out that she had paid the rent but that it had been continually repaid into her account. The estate manager had apologised, explained that it was a computer-generated letter and said that she should just ignore it. He had turned down her offer to write a cheque to cover the rent arrears then and there, and had said something about that not being Mr Dionides's wish. Advising her to ignore any similar letters that she received, he had shown her to the door. When she'd mentioned the matter to Atreus, it had been evident he already knew about it. He had told her not to worry about an oversight made by a new member of staff and that the problem would not arise again.

Now those recollections could only send a shiver down Lindy's tense spine. She thought it very probable that Atreus would prefer her to vacate The Lodge now that their affair was over. Had he sunk low enough to use those supposed rent arrears as an excuse to evict her?

Truly taken aback by that suspicion, Lindy sat down to reread the letter, which was written in clear language and even gave the final date by which she was to vacate the premises. It also said that if she was prepared to leave ahead of that date her rent arrears would be reduced accordingly. It was that last point which confirmed Lindy's sinking suspicion that Atreus simply wanted her off his country estate as soon as possible, and that realisation was just another kick in the teeth.

Indeed, Lindy felt utterly overwhelmed by that final blow, which struck at the very base of her security. She knew that she ought to consult a solicitor, but she also knew just how pricey legal assistance could be. If she was going to be forced to move out she would need every penny she had to secure new accommodation and relocate. And if Atreus was so determined to get rid of her, did she really want to fight to stay? Or to run the risk of having her affair with Atreus alluded to within the public arena of the County Court? After all, her relationship with Atreus and his double-dealing with her rental payments would be central to any defence she attempted to mount. She shuddered at the prospect, but the concept of staying on at The Lodge when her presence there was evidently so very unwelcome was no more appealing.

She loved her compact home, and it provided a perfect base for her business. She had enough land to grow lavender and roses, and the cellar was ideal for the equipment required for pot pourri preparation and candle-making, as well as for the storage and packing of her products. Where else would she find such a base at an affordable rent? It would also be a rare rental property that allowed both the running of a business and the keeping of pets. She fondled Sausage's fluffy ears while the tears trickled down her cheeks. As if that frightening letter were not enough, she also felt sick once more. What a louse Atreus was, and what a rotten, selfish, ruthless rat he was proving to be! No, he had not been joking all those months ago when he had warned her that the creed of the gentleman was long dead. Now that he had decided he no longer wanted her around, Atreus wanted to throw her off his country estate like so much rubbish!

It was in that wretched mood that Lindy phoned her friend Elinor. This time Lindy was too upset to hold anything back, and the whole story came tumbling out, laced with tears and regrets and disbelief that anyone she loved could be treating her so badly. Elinor, who was now the epitome of a very sedate royal princess, residing in Quaram, her husband's country, said some very blunt and unprincesslike things about Atreus, while adding that Lindy was to stop worrying because she already had the perfect solution in mind. Lindy came off the phone feeling reassured and less fearful, although she could not really have said why since she could not see what Elinor could realistically do to help from thousands of miles away.

But that same evening, her other close friend Alissa phoned, and explained that Elinor had consulted her. Alissa immediately offered Lindy the use of a vacant cottage on the country estate which her husband, Sergei Antonovich, had recently bought as a home for his family in the UK.

'I can't let you do that,' Lindy told Alissa ruefully.

'Of course you can. It would be wonderful to be able to see you more often. Did I mention that it's much closer to London as well? And much nearer Elinor's place too. Sergei says that good tenants are really hard to find these days and you'd be very welcome, dogs included. Say yes, Lindy, please,' Alissa pleaded. 'I'm pregnant again, and I would love the company when Sergei's away on business.'

Lindy's eyes stung with tears at the warmth of that request. Her hormones seemed to be operating on a supercharged level, for her emotions were seesawing all over the place and tears flowed more readily to her eyes than they ever had before. It was that acknowledgement which made her decide that possibly she ought to consult the doctor, in case there was something more serious wrong with her than the persistent tummy bug that had not stopped troubling her.

In bed that night she burned with so much anger against Atreus that she could not sleep. He might be about to get his wish to see her move off his exclusive turf, but she wanted him to know what she thought of his despicable methods for achieving his own ends. In the darkness she sat up and put on the light to reset her alarm clock. Tomorrow, she decided, she would catch the train to London in order to see Atreus one more time, before she wiped him out of her mind and her heart for ever!

Atreus frowned when he learned that Lindy was waiting outside his office.

What was her game? What could have persuaded her to come all the way to London to see him? He did not want a scene caused at his place of work. Dionides Shipping was a conservative environment, and Atreus had always kept his private life rigidly separate from his working day. His even white teeth clenching, he caught a glimpse of the wary way his PA was regarding him—an unwelcome reminder that for the past few weeks Atreus had been struggling to control a disturbing tendency to explode into anger in a way that was far from being the norm for him.

Lush black lashes screened Atreus's brilliant dark eyes and concealed his bewilderment at his own behaviour. When, he wondered in frustration, could he expect to return to feeling like himself again? Whatever, he had no choice but to see Lindy and draw a line under that unfortunate affair. He was already seeing how an unconventional relationship with someone who did not belong to his world could have unexpected and destructive repercussions. It was a lesson his foolish father had never learned, and Atreus had no intention of following in his late parent's footsteps.

Lindy was trembling when she walked into Atreus's big, imposing office. She had got out of bed at dawn to ensure she was well groomed, because there could be no satisfaction in suspecting that he might be looking at her and marvelling at how he had ever got involved with her in the first place. With her hair tamed into a blade-straight fall and a light application of make-up, wearing a burgundy blouse teamed with a pencil skirt and a smart knitted jacket, she felt strong enough to confront him.

Atreus sprang upright, his tall, powerful physique sheathed in a perfectly tailored black pinstripe business suit. He studied her, immediately aware of the impact of her soft pink-glossed mouth, the even more tempting swell of her full breasts below her shirt and the violin curve of her hips. His reaction to her appeal was instant and earthy, and it infuriated him to have so little control over his libido. There was a decided touch of sarcasm in his tone when he asked coolly, 'How may I help you?'

And, that fast, Lindy wanted to hit him. There he stood, looking absolutely gorgeous the way he always did, and how dared he address her as if she was an importunate stranger? How dared he look down on her from his intimidating height with that hateful aloof expression when it was only days since they had made love? That, it seemed, was an injudicious recollection, for her eyes stung hotly when she finally acknowledged that they had not made love. It took two people to make love. Atreus had only been having sex: casual, uncommitted, very physical sex.

Lindy walked right to the edge of his desk and slapped the Notice to Quit she had received the day before down in front of him. 'I wanted to hand this back to you personally,' she informed him with gutsy calm, her dark brown hair flipping back like heavy silk from her flushed face, her blue eyes very bright. 'I did nothing to deserve this kind of treatment. If I'd known eighteen months ago what I know about you now, we would never have had a relationship. You're a man without conscience and a horrible bully!'

Astonished by that censorious attack, Atreus

was studying the document she had received. 'I did not authorise this!' he proclaimed in angry rebuttal.

'Didn't you? But you do want me off your estate, don't you?' Lindy noted the faint hint of colour that accentuated his wonderful cheekbones. 'What gives you the right to disrupt my whole life? Where did you think I was going to move to on my income, with two dogs and a business to house as well as myself?' A scornful laugh fell from her lips. 'Of course—the point is that you didn't care.'

'I have no intention of evicting you for non-payment of rent,' Atreus ground out in an accented drawl that was roughened with scantily controlled rage. 'In the circumstances that is a ridiculous charge—and someone will lose their job over this…'

'Your estate manager, who has four kids and another on the way?' Lindy fired back at him in unconcealed disgust. 'Atreus, you made this situation. Don't make someone else pay the price for it going wrong. He's an employee who is clearly aware that you want me to leave the estate.'

Atreus sent her a fierce appraisal. 'I was willing to offer you generous financial compensation for simply considering the prospect of moving.'

'So your estate manager probably thought he would win brownie points with you by getting rid of me on the cheap.' Lindy shrugged, the generous curve of her lips compressing to a thin line. 'That doesn't free you of the responsibility for the distress and inconvenience that I have been caused.'

Irate at finding himself in the position of being reproved for his behaviour, Atreus held up two hands to still the flood of condemnation flowing from her. 'You're not listening to me. I deeply regret any distress that has been caused, but this was not a mistake of my making.'

Lindy shook her head unimpressed. 'You don't think so? You're a ruthless bastard, Atreus. You have a God-given belief in your right to put your wishes above everyone else's, no matter how selfish or wrong you are in principle. Oh, yes, that's one more thing you lack—principles…'

Atreus stared back at her with chilling intensity. 'You are here to strike back at me because I walked out on you at the weekend?'

It was Lindy's turn to get mad. 'No, I am not!' she protested, her eyes brightening with fury. 'I just wanted you to know what I think of you, because I won't agree to see you or speak to you again if you get down on your knees and beg!'

'Message received, but the scenario you suggest is highly unlikely to happen,' Atreus derided, soft as silk. 'However, you may disregard this foolish document and make your own decision about where you live and do business without any fear of interference from me or from any of my employees.'

'It's too late for that. Ironically, you're going to get what you want—I'm moving out just as soon as it can be arranged,' Lindy admitted tightly. 'I'm lucky that I have some real friends, who don't feel the need to use the power of their wealth and position to persecute people who dare to annoy them!'

His lean, darkly handsome features set hard, Atreus strode round his desk. 'What a drama queen you can be!' he condemned. 'How can you possibly accuse me of persecuting you?'

Lindy was recalling his pronounced air of detachment when she had first entered his office, and the turmoil of her teeming thoughts suddenly fixed on the recognition of one deeply unsettling and wounding fact. 'I can see now that you were never comfortable with being involved with me. I didn't fit, I didn't match your high expectations, and I was never good enough in your eyes to be anything other than a mistress. I will never forgive you for the way you have treated me.'

An ebony brow quirked. 'I'd like to get back to work now…if you're finished?'

And all the way back home on the train his unemotional parting words haunted Lindy. How could she still be so in love with a man like that? And how could he be so horribly, hatefully indifferent to her? But she had no regrets about having paid him a visit. This time he knew how she felt, and she could only hope that something of what she had said stayed with him.

The following day Lindy went to see her doctor. She was sent to the nurse for tests and sat around afterwards in the waiting room, feeling dreadfully tired and nauseous again even though she had been sick earlier that morning.

When she was called back in the doctor had a shock in store for her.

'You're pregnant,' she was told.

Her response to the doctor was that it was totally impossible! The doctor looked weary, as though he had heard that claim before, and asked to examine her while making enquiries as to her menstrual cycle. It was true that she'd felt her system was a little out of kilter, she acknowledged, but she argued that no risks at all had been taken. The doctor cheerfully pointed out that certain unmistakable changes were already taking place in her body, and informed her that it was possible to have an unusually light period in the early stages of conception, before the pregnancy hormones fully kicked in. By the time he had told her that condoms could have up to a twelve percent failure rate in the first year of use, she was beginning to sink into the shock of acceptance.

She drove home with care, struggling to adapt to the reality that she and Atreus had quarrelled bitterly and broken up while all the time a tiny new life was growing inside her womb. Her sense of wonder and warmth towards that little being was soon disrupted by less pleasant feelings. Atreus didn't want her and he would certainly not want her baby. The knowledge chilled her, but Atreus had been brutally frank on the subject of children. He would only consider having a family when he was married—to a suitably rich Greek woman.

Alissa rang to chat at length about her plans for Lindy's move, and midway through the conversation Lindy blurted out that she too was expecting a child.

'My goodness! Have you told Atreus?'

Lindy explained in some detail why nothing would persuade her to organise such a ghastly confrontation. 'I couldn't face it—not knowing that he doesn't want the baby or me.'

'The sooner you move the better,' her friend commented soothingly. 'Don't worry about it. You don't need Atreus Dionides any more.'

Lying in her bed that night, Lindy tried to convince herself of the same fact, drumming up a recollection of Atreus's every masculine flaw and telling herself that she would be a much happier person without him. Unfortunately she could only remember how happy she had been while she was with him, even if that happiness had been built on shaky foundations. But she knew she was a survivor and that Atreus had been a bad choice, different as he was in every way from her.

That acknowledgement made and accepted, Lindy splayed her fingers protectively over her slightly rounded tummy and allowed herself to think of how comforting it would be to see Elinor and Alissa on a more regular basis. She wanted her baby. She wanted her baby very much, even though she was worried sick about how she would manage to raise a child alone, without a father's support.

CHAPTER SEVEN

'YOU'RE selling a country fantasy along with your products,' Alissa pointed out, rearranging the skirt of Lindy's floral sundress on the summer swing seat on which she was reclining, with a pretty basket of freshly cut lavender by her side. 'Your customers want to believe you are living that fantasy.'

Before the hovering photographer could zoom in to take another photo of her Lindy pushed herself up heavily on her elbows, gasping at the effort it took to rise from a supine position since she had lost the ability to bend in the middle. The baby bump had taken over, and even a pretty dress and professional make-up couldn't make her feel attractive when the solid mound of her pregnant tummy reminded her of a Himalayan peak.

It had never occurred to her that her accidental pregnancy might coincide with one of the hardest working periods of her life. But that was how it had turned out in the four months that had passed since she had left the Chantry estate. Having taken up residence in an idyllic and recently renovated thatched cottage, complete with a couple of acres of ground, Lindy had begun to calculate how she could make her business more lucrative and therefore more secure for her child's sake. Idle conversations on that score with Atreus had long ago ensured that she knew exactly where she was going wrong in her pursuit of profit. Atreus had told her she needed an upmarket catalogue and fancier packaging, and she had now followed through on that useful advice. Alissa's husband, Sergei, had insisted that even the smallest business required publicity to sell its products, hence the interview she had given earlier that day, and the photographer now snapping fluffy shots of her, the dogs and the beautiful garden.

There was no fantasy in her world now, Lindy conceded ruefully. It had taken a lot of concealer to hide the big dark shadows below her eyes from sleepless nights. In the months since they had parted Atreus had been seen out and about with an ever-changing collection of women, and rarely with the same one twice. Recently, however, that had changed. Just weeks back Atreus had been photographed dining out with an extremely eligible Greek heiress, who…yes…naturally was tiny and very beautiful. The gossip columnists had got very excited and had wasted little time in forecasting wedding bells for so well-matched a pair.

Lindy had honestly believed she was fully recovered from Atreus until Alissa had passed her a glossy magazine containing an article that made it very clear, to Lindy at least that, Atreus was indeed thinking of marrying Krista Perris. Lindy had been very brave about the news while she had an audience, but had wept buckets once she was alone. It had hurt so much to see Krista and Atreus pictured together in a full colour spread in that magazine. Krista, heiress to another shipping fortune, was so patently perfect for him in every way. Elinor's husband, Prince Jasim, had urged Lindy to waste no more time in getting in touch with Atreus and telling him that she was pregnant, and Sergei had even offered to tell Atreus personally—an offer Lindy had hastily declined, reckoning that the Russian billionaire would pull few punches at such a meeting.

In a move that had convinced Lindy that Atreus was serious about Krista, Atreus had taken Krista home to meet his family. The picture of Atreus and his beautiful petite heiress heading into a party being thrown by his relatives had hurt Lindy the most. After all, it was an honour that he had never considered Lindy worthy of receiving. There was no way that Lindy wanted to pop up right now, with a big pregnant tummy, to break news that would scandalise the Dionides and the Perris families, appal Atreus and devastate his bride-to-be.

Lindy was far too proud and independent to stage such a tasteless denouement. She was getting by fine without Atreus and would continue to do so. To be happy at the same time was expecting too much of herself. As far as possible she was concentrating on her business and the child she carried, and she never, ever consciously allowed herself to think about Atreus Dionides. With the single exception of the baby, Atreus had been a mistake—the biggest mistake she had ever made.

Woken from her sleep at an unusually early hour for a Sunday morning, Lindy sat staring aghast at the double-page spread in the tabloid newspaper. It was luridly entitled 'Tycoon's Secret Mistress and Child'.

'This is my worst nightmare!' she gasped, stricken, while she studied the photo of her that appeared in the catalogue which innocently advertised her business. 'How on earth did they get hold of this stuff?'

Alissa, who had seated herself at the foot of the bed, groaned. 'It looks like someone who knew you when you were living on the Chantry House estate put two and two together and decided to talk to the press—probably for a pay-off.'

Even before she'd read the accompanying text Lindy had broken out in a cold sweat. But when she digested an account of her relationship with Atreus in which she was described as a 'weekend mistress', and their sudden split was mentioned, together with hints that rumours of her pregnancy had circulated even before her departure from Chantry, her blood boiled with angry mortification. It was even more humiliating to see herself depicted side by side with a gorgeous picture of the ultimate size-zero hottie and heiress Krista Perris.

Her mobile phone started buzzing like an angry wasp on the bedside table, and after a moment of hesitation she snatched it up.

Shock paralysed her when she heard Atreus's rich, dark accented drawl.

'Have you seen the article in the *Sunday Voice*?' Atreus enquired with freezing bite.

'Er…yes.'

'I'm flying down to see you to deal with this. I'll be with you in just over an hour.'

'I don't want you to come here—to my home—I really don't want to talk to you, either!' Lindy argued vehemently.

'I didn't offer you a choice,' Atreus asserted, and the phone line went dead as he hung up on her.

Alissa frowned when Lindy informed her of Atreus's plans. 'It may not be what you want, but you do need to sort things out with him, Lindy.'

'Why?' Lindy manoeuvred her heavy body out of her comfortable bed and turned angry blue eyes full of enquiry on her friend. 'After the way he behaved, I don't owe him anything. And you and Elinor agreed with me!'

'In the heat of the moment. I hate to admit it, but it was Jasim who made me stop and think.

He's always so level-headed. Even if you don't feel you have a claim on Atreus Dionides, your baby does, and it's much wiser to get this out into the open now, rather than try to keep it a secret. On the face of it, the press have done that for you.'

Trembling with alarm, and a shameful sense of anticipation at the prospect of seeing Atreus again, Lindy breathed in deeply to steady herself. It had not yet occurred to her to think of her unborn child as an individual, with the right to seek an independent relationship with Atreus at some point in the future. Alissa's reminder had sobered Lindy, however, and forced her to acknowledge how complicated the issue of her child's paternity would become if she did not deal honestly with it in the present.

'There are reporters waiting out on the main road,' Alissa told her. 'If you want to go out, I'd advise using the farm lane.'

'Thanks for the warning. I need a shower.' Lindy sighed, and headed in the direction of the bathroom.

'I'll stay a minute and pick out something for you to wear.'

'Where are the children?' Lindy was belatedly noticing the absence of Alissa and Sergei's lively toddler, Evelina, and their six-week-old baby boy, Alek.

'I left them with Sergei.'

Having witnessed Sergei in the role of child-carer when Alissa was recovering from giving birth to their son and their nanny had fallen ill, Lindy was surprised. Before Lindy had taken charge Sergei had tried to hand his newborn son a bottle, and had given Evelina a packet of biscuits instead of a meal.

'He has to learn how to handle them some time, and he assured me he would manage fine,' Alissa quipped, with the smile of a woman who liked to see her husband occasionally faced with the challenges of child-care.

Lindy ignored the pretty feminine outfit which Alissa had selected for her to wear and went for an embroidered black skirt and a black camisole top, both of which she was convinced minimised the size of her stomach. By the time she heard the noisy clatter of a helicopter approaching she was extremely tense. She let the dogs out, not wanting the fuss of their greeting Atreus indoors.

The helicopter bore a large scarlet Dionides logo, and it landed in the paddock next to her cottage. From upstairs, her heart beating very fast, she watched Atreus's bodyguards emerge first and check the surrounding area before their employer appeared. The dogs circumvented the efforts of the bodyguards to head them off and hurled themselves at Atreus with joyful jumping abandon. No doubt he would be a little less immaculate than he usually was when he finally fought free and reached her doorstep, Lindy reflected, without even a small stab of conscience. She hated him, she totally and absolutely hated the man she had once loved because of the power he still had to hurt her.

In the act of brushing his suit free of dog hairs and muddy pawprints, Atreus saw Lindy in the doorway, blue eyes violet-bright and the summer sunlight picking up the sheen of her chestnut-coloured hair, which had grown in length since he'd last seen her and now fell well past her shoulders. Bitter icy-cold anger engulfed him, because he had always trusted her and had never dreamt that she might pull such a stunt on him.

'If we had to see each other I would rather it hadn't been here. This is my home,' Lindy told him with quiet dignity. 'And you're spoiling my Sunday. You're going to make me late for church.'

Atreus was distracted by her concluding comment, snatched back to the weekends when he had regarded keeping her in bed with him rather than rushing off to church as the ultimate challenge.

'Who sold the story to the *Sunday Voice*?' he queried, before he had even entered the cottage.

His lean bronzed features were cool and grim, but he could not conceal the hot angry gold of his arrogant gaze. He was still the most beautiful man she had ever seen, and the admission annoyed her—for she felt that a truly intelligent woman would by now be indifferent to his vibrant dark good-looks.

'How would I know?' Lindy riposted. 'Lots of people knew about us in the village, even though they said nothing to my face. Everybody on the estate knew as well. We weren't exactly the world's biggest secret.'

'So, you're saying that *you* didn't sell it?' Atreus caught a sideways glimpse of her altered shape and stared at the fecund swell of her stomach with frowning force. There was certainly no doubt that she was pregnant.

Shifting uncomfortably beneath that stare, Lindy shot him a furious glance. 'No, indeed I did not. I'm not short of money, and I wouldn't sell details of my private life even if I was!'

Atreus was treating the elegant modern fittings of the living room to a curious appraisal. 'This seems to be a comfortable house.'

'It is. Alissa oversaw the renovation project for all the buildings on the estate, and she never does anything by halves,' she advanced. 'If you've come all the way here to accuse me of giving the press that story, I can assure you that you're barking up the wrong tree. I had nothing to gain and everything to lose from that article appearing in print because I value my privacy.'

Razor-sharp dark golden eyes scanned her angry resentful expression. 'I didn't come here to argue with you.'

'No?' Elevating a brow and standing her ground, Lindy looked unimpressed by that claim.

'No,' Atreus framed flatly. 'But I am very angry that such an outrageous account of our relationship has been published and I intend to sue.'

'Good for you,' Lindy pronounced, tongue in cheek. 'No doubt you'll win, and six months from now, when everyone has long since forgotten the original article, the newspaper will print a retraction low down on some boring page where virtually no one will even notice it or read it. Is it really worth all that hassle?'

Her mockery made his black brows draw together. 'It's not quite that simple. My family in Greece will be very much shocked by that item…' He cloaked his stunning eyes with dense black lashes. 'You may not be aware of it, but I have been thinking of getting engaged…'

Lindy wrinkled her nose. 'Too much information, Atreus,' she said, very drily.

Atreus threw back his wide powerful shoulders as if he was bracing himself to continue. 'What I intended to say, if you had not interrupted me, is that this story is a source of embarrassment for Krista, the woman I'm currently seeing, and to her family and friends as well. We are not the only people affected by what appeared in the newspaper today.'

Lindy was feeling sick with tension, and listening to Atreus talk about the effect of that article on Krista only made her feel worse than ever. Had he ever cared about her that way? For even a moment? Had he even thought of how performing this knight on a white horse act on Krista's behalf might make Lindy feel? But then why should he think or even care now? His indifference was like a knife twisting inside her, and she was defenceless against the pain of it.

She shook her head, the shiny strands of rich brown hair rippling across her slim shoulders. 'I really don't know what you're doing here.'

'I want you to agree to make a statement that the child you are carrying is not mine. Just to set the record straight for us all,' Atreus completed, smooth as silk. 'I have brought one of my company lawyers here with me. He's waiting in the helicopter and will advise you on the correct wording.'

Astonished by his request, Lindy stared back into level dark golden eyes and felt her heart breaking inside her. All of a sudden she was wondering if everyone had been right when they'd advised her to set aside her own feelings and tell Atreus that she was pregnant as soon as possible. She had waited, kept silent, and now an awful lot of water had passed under the proverbial bridge. His life had moved on to a fresh chapter that had no place for her in any capacity.

'You're so organised,' Lindy remarked stiffly, moving away from him to stare out of the window. Far from impervious to her tension, the dogs nudged against her legs and Sausage released an anxious whine. 'It's all right,' she told the elderly dog, reaching down somewhat awkwardly to pat his shaggy head. 'I'm fine.'

'Lindy…' Atreus let her name trail off. 'The rumours set off by that article will be repeated again in the future if action isn't taken against them now.'

Colour flaring over her cheekbones, Lindy spun back—or at least she tried. But she had moved too fast, and her sense of balance was no longer reliable. As her head swam she clutched at the back of the chair next to her, to steady legs that felt as safe and dependable as bendy twigs.

It came as a complete shock when Atreus strode forward to close a supportive arm round her. 'Are you all right?'

'No,' she said a little shrilly, in growing distress at the situation in which she found herself. 'Anything but.'

The disturbingly familiar scent of his skin, his hair and his cologne was washing over her and arousing agonisingly acute slivers of intimate memory. She remembered him too well, and she stiffened in consternation when her body reacted accordingly. Her breasts swelled and tightened inside her bra, while a sliding sensation of warm awareness stirred between her thighs. She drove out that humiliating sexual awareness with an image of Krista Perris, with her long blonde hair, tiny designer-clad body and cute smile: the woman he was thinking of marrying. The effort of it almost broke her in two. Pulling away from him in an abrupt movement, she slid a seeking hand down to the arm of the chair and sank heavily down into it.

'You've wasted your time coming down here with your lawyer in tow,' she murmured between compressed lips. 'I can't help you.'

'You mean, you won't help me?' Atreus gritted, his exasperation unhidden.

Lindy lifted her head. 'Just whose baby do you think this is?'

Atreus shrugged. 'That's none of my business. I merely want a statement from you to tidy this up, so that neither I nor my family will be haunted by unsavoury rumours of an illegitimate child for years into the future,' he completed impatiently.

Lindy threaded slim fingers unsteadily through the hair tumbling over her warm brow. A little more stable in body now that she was seated, she was fumbling for the right words but already regretting the fact that she had remained silent about her pregnancy for so many months. Her secrecy had left him horribly unprepared for the announcement she now had to make.

'I can't agree to make that statement for you

because I would be telling a lie,' Lindy explained with care. 'I know you don't want to hear this right now, Atreus…but this is your baby.'

His eyes narrowed, his lean strong face tightening, his jawline taking on an aggressive slant. 'That's not possible.'

'There's no such thing as one hundred per cent reliable birth control,' Lindy countered. 'Somehow it went wrong for us.'

'I don't believe this. You staged this vulgar press exposure to try and con me into believing that this is my child?'

Lindy's hands closed tight on the chair-arms so that she could lever herself upright again. 'That's the end of our little talk, Atreus. I want you to leave now.' She walked briskly to the front door and yanked it open with the suggestion of suppressed violence.

'This is ridiculous. You can't throw a bombshell like that at me and then demand that I leave without explaining yourself,' Atreus ground out, dark golden eyes censorious and hot as molten metal.

'The first point I would like to make is that I don't have anything to explain. The second is that I will not tolerate being accused of trying to con you or anyone else. You got me pregnant—deal with it!' Lindy slung back at him in furious challenge.

Brilliant dark eyes fringed by inky lashes fiercely focused on her, Atreus closed his hands over hers. 'I don't want to set my lawyers on you, Lindy—I only want to know why you're doing this…'

Lindy forcefully wrenched her fingers free of his hold. 'How dare you? You hounded me out of my home, you disrupted my whole life, and you got me pregnant! Now you're threatening me with your lawyers?'

'Nobody's going to threaten you,' another voice cut in, with rasping bite.

Atreus and Lindy swung round. Sergei Antonovich was poised several feet away. 'Alissa has been worried about you and it seems she had good cause.'

When he saw the other man, Atreus became

so tense he might have been chipped out of solid granite. 'Sergei,' he acknowledged grittily. 'I appreciate your concern, but we don't need an audience right now.'

The Russian tycoon sent Lindy a questioning glance. 'If legal advice is required, you will have full access to any assistance you need.'

'Thank you,' Lindy breathed, tears prickling behind her eyes, because Sergei and Alissa had been so very kind and supportive when she was at her lowest ebb, and she really appreciated that. 'But you don't need to stay.'

Lindy stepped back indoors and wished she had controlled her temper enough to have stayed there in the first instance. Fighting with Atreus or letting other people get involved in what was a hugely private issue would only exacerbate the tensions between them. Leaving Atreus to follow her, Lindy moved back into the living room and resisted a provocative urge to ask him if Krista Perris knew where he was. 'Would you like coffee?'

'Yes. Exactly when did you get so friendly with Antonovich?'

'He owns this place. My friendship is with his wife, Alissa. I have mentioned her to you several times. Alissa and I shared a flat a few years ago.'

'I didn't make the correct connection.'

Atreus watched her switch on the kettle in the light-filled kitchen. He breathed in slow and deep, studying her taut profile and the unfamiliar shape of her pregnant body. His baby? The thought struck him hard. Accidents happened. He knew that—of course he did. But how could any man know whose baby it was inside a woman? And, having been burned more than once by allegations, he was more suspicious and cynical than other men.

'Is it my baby?' he prompted, in a driven undertone.

'Yes. It's your baby,' Lindy confirmed heavily. 'And you don't have any excuse that I know of to even ask me that question.'

'Halliwell's bow-tie was lying on your

bedroom floor the last time we slept together,' Atreus shared flatly.

Taken aback, Lindy studied him. 'That was the night Ben and I went to a wedding party at Headby Hall. I let him have the bed and I slept on the sofa,' she explained slowly. 'You never mentioned the bow-tie at the time…'

His lean dark features hardened. 'I didn't see the point.'

'I'm carrying your child. I expect you to trust me when I tell you something.'

'That's a tall order for me,' Atreus admitted.

'You expected me to trust you when you were photographed in the company of other women in London during our relationship,' Lindy reminded him darkly.

Challenged, Atreus shrugged a magnificent shoulder and sipped his black coffee. 'I've never lied to you.'

'DNA tests can be dangerous during pregnancy.' Lindy spoke in a curt, harried tone. 'I won't risk a miscarriage just to satisfy your lack of faith in my word.'

Atreus set his even white teeth together and said nothing.

In the uneasy silence Lindy began talking quickly and quietly. 'I was ten weeks pregnant before I found out. We'd already broken up. Right from the start I knew I wanted this baby, but that you wouldn't.'

'You had no right to make such assumptions.'

'Assumptions based on fact. You had already told me that you didn't want a baby with me, and that you would only want one when you were married,' Lindy pointed out doggedly. 'So, based on those comments, I naturally made the assumption that you would want me to either have a termination or hand over my child for adoption.'

'*Never*!' Atreus bit out rawly. 'Never would I have suggested such a solution!'

'Well, I wasn't drawn to those options either, and I couldn't see any point in lowering myself to tell you that I had conceived,' she admitted tautly.

His dark golden eyes were bleak. 'In what way would you have been lowering yourself?'

Lindy recalled how she had felt when they broke up, and how much worse she had felt after that final time when they had shared the same bed. She swallowed hard. 'You hurt me a lot. That Notice to Quit I received was the last straw. I just couldn't face having anything more to do with you.'

Incensed with her version of womanly logic, Atreus swore in Greek under his breath. 'Even though you knew I wasn't behind that debacle over you staying on at The Lodge?'

'No, but you wanted me gone—out of sight, out of mind. I saw that in you,' Lindy condemned quietly. 'I didn't feel that I could afford to depend on you.'

Atreus almost groaned aloud. She saw all that was worst in him and concentrated on that. He knew he was not perfect. He knew he was not a saint. But he would never have walked away had he known that she needed him, and he was insulted that she could have thought otherwise. Suddenly he felt confined in the small room. He had a deep craving for the energising light and burn of a hotter sun on his body, for the timeless beat of the Aegean waves on the shore on his private island of Thrazos, where he could be himself.

'You weren't fair to me,' he told her boldly. 'You didn't give me a chance.'

'Well, it doesn't matter now. Life has moved on for both of us.' Lindy forced a determined smile onto her strained face. 'Look, all this has been a shock to you. Why don't you leave so that you can work out how you feel about the situation? Then we can talk.'

'Some things I already know. If your baby is mine, I cannot possibly consider marrying another woman.' Pale and taut beneath his bronzed complexion, Atreus settled glittering dark, steady eyes on Lindy's startled expression. 'What sort of a man do you think I am? I could not turn my back on you or my child. In those circumstances both of you would have first claim on my loyalty and support.'

Rocked by his confirmation of the fact that he had been thinking of marrying Krista Perris, Lindy folded her arms in a defensive movement. 'I don't want any sort of a claim on you. I don't want to mess up anyone else's life—yours or your girlfriend's.'

His lean strong face had a stern aspect. 'There's nothing you can do. Things are already messed up and we can't change that, but we can do what has to be done for the child's sake.'

'My life is fine just the way it is at the minute,' Lindy protested. 'I have a business, a healthy income, and somewhere secure to live. I don't need anything else. I don't need your loyalty or your support—it's too late for all that.'

'It's not too late for the baby.'

'You don't even want the baby!' Lindy hurled at him in bewilderment. 'For goodness' sake, you've already admitted that you're on the brink of asking another woman to marry you!'

Atreus gave her a grim look. 'But I want my baby to have everything I didn't have. A normal home, loving parents, a solid knowledge of who he or she is, and security. If I marry another woman the child won't have those essentials, and I owe my own flesh and blood more than that.'

Oxygen feathered in Lindy's dry throat as she finally appreciated that he no longer doubted her. 'So you accept that I'm telling the truth and that this is your baby?'

His rare charismatic smile momentarily lightened the hard set of his wide sensual mouth. 'When did you ever lie to me?'

It was a small confirmation of the trust they had once shared, and it almost brought tears to her eyes. It was a relief that he did not still doubt her claim that he had fathered her child. She twisted her head away and dropped it to stare at her linked hands. It was news to her that Atreus had not benefited from a secure home with loving parents. He never mentioned his childhood, but she was aware that both his father and mother had been dead for a good number of years.

'So you really want to play a role in this child's life?' Lindy prompted uncertainly.

His lean strong face clenched. 'I want more than that. But we can discuss that some other time, when you look less tired.'

Lindy did not appreciate his assurance that she looked tired. Unfortunately emotional stress and tension always exhausted her, and although the nausea she had suffered no longer bothered her, she was still waiting to enjoy the reputed 'glow' of pregnancy. 'I don't want us to be enemies.'

'You don't need to worry about that. This pregnancy may be an unforeseen development,' Atreus drawled softly, 'but, as you'll discover, I can roll with the punches.'

'Not perhaps the most tactful euphemism you could have used to reassure me,' Lindy quipped wryly, looking up at him and noting how the sunshine gleamed over his black hair, warming his bronzed skin and accentuating the stunning gold of his eyes. For a split second, before she got her control back in place, she craved his touch with every fibre of her being.

'I'm in shock,' Atreus confided ruefully. 'I'll get over it, though. This baby will change everything.'

Lindy appreciated his honesty, but it hurt. She didn't know what she expected from him any more. In his swift acceptance of her condition and his paternity he had exceeded her expectations, but nothing could stop her reflecting that her revelation was already threatening to turn his life upside down. He insisted that he wanted a role in their child's life. He had said that he couldn't marry Krista now...

Was that because he knew his gorgeous girlfriend would not accept a husband who came with the baggage of an acknowledged illegitimate child? How did he really feel inside? Was he in love with Krista? And would their relationship continue even though they didn't marry? Recognising that she wanted answers to questions that were really no longer any of her business, Lindy suppressed her teeming thoughts. One problem that she did fully acknowledge was that she was still too vulnerable to Atreus. She needed to guard against that weakness and learn how to keep her distance—mentally and physically.

CHAPTER EIGHT

FORTY-EIGHT hours later, Atreus was shown out of Krista's apartment by her maid. His lean, darkly handsome face was grim with suppressed emotion. He was angry with everything and everyone, himself included. He thought he was very probably angry with the whole world, and it was not a mood he wanted to inflict on Lindy. Drawing out his mobile phone, he rearranged their meeting for the following morning.

'Are you all right?' Lindy heard herself ask, catching an odd note in his deep voice that disturbed her.

'Why wouldn't I be?' Atreus suppressed a groan at that query and compressed his handsome mouth hard. 'I'm sorry for the last-minute change of plan.'

Grimacing at her slip in asking such a personal question, and with her cheeks burning, Lindy hastened to say as casually as she could, 'It's not a problem.'

At her end of the phone she glanced in the hall mirror and winced. Hair tamed within an inch of its life: check. Full make-up: check. New outfit calculated to make the most of what shape she retained: check. Did she never learn? Why was she doing this to herself?

She walked back into the living room, where the remnants of a light lunch remained on the dining table and exchanged a rueful smile with her guest. 'Atreus just cancelled,' she shared.

'Oh, dear…' Princess Elinor of Quaram, a willowy redhead who had been on the brink of leaving, sat down again and occupied herself by brushing her younger son's hair off his brow. Tarif, a cute-as-a-button toddler with his father's black hair and his mother's light eyes, returned to the toys he had been playing with. 'That's unfortunate.'

'It's not like him. Something must have

come up,' Lindy declared, watching her friend's older boy, Sami, and her daughter, Mariyah, flying a kite in the paddock with the help of their tall, athletic father. 'But I'm not bothered. I'm being sensible now, and I'm over Atreus.'

Her companion gave her a doubtful appraisal.

'No, seriously—I am over him,' Lindy emphasised.

'If you say so,' Elinor said mildly. 'But I think you've had a traumatic time over the last few months. Don't rush into making any big decisions.'

Lindy struggled to stay calm while she waited for Atreus's arrival the next morning. He was the father of her baby and otherwise no big deal, she told herself earnestly. All right, so he was gorgeous, but he was with another woman now, and her only remaining connection with him was an inconvenient pregnancy. She watched him pull up outside in a gleaming black Bugatti Veyron and she made herself hang back and count slowly to ten before she went to open the front door.

Atreus thrust a bouquet of roses into her arms. Startled by that almost awkward gesture from a man who had never given her flowers even when they were lovers, Lindy muttered her thanks. Flustered, she abandoned him to go off and put the flowers in water.

Curiously untroubled by the scent of lavender in the cottage, Atreus paced the wood floor, impatient for her return.

In full polite hostess mode, Lindy reappeared with a tray of coffee and biscuits for him, and homemade lemonade for herself. 'My business is doing very well at present,' she told him proudly.

Atreus tensed. 'There's a lot of physical labour involved in your business. I'd like to hire someone to take care of that side of your work.'

'I don't need any help. I'm not sick or delicate, just pregnant.'

'I talked to a friend who's a doctor. He said

that heavy work is not a good idea at this point in your pregnancy.'

Her teeth closed together with a snap. 'I think that's my affair.'

Brilliant dark eyes clashed with hers head-on. 'Not when you're carrying my baby.'

The speed with which he voiced that direct challenge for supremacy shook Lindy, who had contrived to forget just how interfering and bossy Atreus could be. She breathed in deep to hang onto her temper, telling herself that it was good that he should take an interest in her health. 'I wouldn't do anything stupid.'

'You might. You don't like accepting help,' Atreus pointed out with infuriating accuracy. 'So recruit an assistant and I'll cover the expense until you're fully fit again.'

Lindy could not breathe in deeply enough to douse the fire of temper he had ignited inside her. 'I appreciate your anxiety, but how I live and how I choose to manage my business is my concern.'

'But you are my concern,' Atreus purred, like a prowling jungle cat.

'Since when?' Lindy challenged.

His dark golden gaze narrowed. 'Since you conceived. If you had told me the day you found that out, we would still be together.'

Lindy veiled her gaze. 'So you say—but then we can all be wise after the event. Five months ago you made it very clear than an unplanned pregnancy would destroy our relationship.'

'After my experiences with women in that field it was second nature for me to talk in that vein. It's what I do now that it's happened that speaks best for me,' Atreus informed her with firm conviction. 'And I'm here today to ask you to be my wife.'

In the act of pouring lemonade into a glass, Lindy switched her attention to him, her violet-blue eyes wide with disbelief. Frozen as she was by shock, she went on pouring the lemonade until the glass overflowed onto the tray beneath. The deluge only stopped when

Atreus strode forward and lifted the jug from her paralysed grasp.

'I don't believe you just said that,' Lindy admitted unevenly.

'You're expecting my child. What could be more natural?'

Lindy dealt him a transfixed appraisal. 'I can't think of anything more *un*natural! We broke up because you spelt out the fact that you would never consider marrying someone like me. What about Krista?'

His strong jaw line hardened. 'That's over and done with.'

'But you were planning to marry her!' Lindy protested.

'Was I?' Atreus treated her to an impassive look that revealed nothing.

'You took her home to meet your family, which for you was quite a statement,' Lindy pronounced, her pride still smarting over the reality that even after eighteen months she had never met a single member of the reclusive Dionides family.

Determined to prevent her from muddying the water with pointless references to Krista, Atreus lifted and dropped a wide shoulder. 'There's little point in discussing what might have been now.'

Sensitive as she was on the issue of Krista Perris, Lindy turned her head away sharply, as if he had slapped her.

'I want to talk about us.'

Lindy almost laughed out loud. 'There is no us. The fact I'm pregnant doesn't wipe out the last few months, or the reasons we split up.'

Atreus breathed in deep. The silence was laden with tension.

'And I'm not interested in playing a role in a shotgun marriage. I suppose I should say thank you for asking,' Lindy replied in a doubtful tone, 'but you thought I was totally unsuitable as a wife when we broke up, and you weren't shy about telling me that. I don't see what's changed.'

Atreus could no longer restrain his ire. 'Look in the mirror. Our baby needs both of us—and in my family we get married when a woman is pregnant.'

'Whatever turns you on.' Lindy grimaced, and closed both hands round her glass of lemonade. 'But I'm afraid it's not something that I could agree to, and I think I'm doing both of us a favour in being the sensible one.'

Atreus regarded her with fulminating eyes. 'What's sensible about it? You will be denying my child my name.'

'That doesn't have to be an issue. If necessary, names can be changed by deed poll,' Lindy informed him.

'Only if we're married can I be a proper father to our child!' Atreus lanced back at her, far from mollified by her prosaic assurance that names could be legally changed outside the bonds of matrimony.

'I think we're both adult enough to know that that's not true. I will be happy for you to take an interest in our child, but we don't need to get our lives tangled up on any other level,' Lindy stated, tilting her chin. 'Let's be honest,

Atreus. You moved on from me pretty quickly, and neither one of us wants to go back.'

Scorching golden eyes clashed with hers. 'Don't tell me what I want. You don't know what I want.'

Lindy thought that getting married to Atreus would be wonderful—but only for a little while. Once the novelty of having a child wore off for him she would be left with an empty marriage and a husband who didn't love her, who had once let her go even though she loved him. The pain of losing Atreus a second time would be more than she could bear, so why put herself through such an ordeal? Just for the short-lived joy of being able to call herself his wife?

'As separate individuals sharing a child we can enjoy a mutually respectful relationship. But if we marry we will just end up getting divorced, because I'm not and will never be the wife you really want,' Lindy told him starkly.

'And how do you make that out?' Atreus demanded rawly, astonished by the barrage of arguments she was employing against him.

'Because you picked Krista Perris, who is everything I am not. She's Greek and she's rich and she's doll-sized. I can't compete and I don't intend to even try.' Strong pride made Lindy lift her head high, for she meant every word that she was saying. She didn't want to be hurt again. She didn't want to be a second-best wife, tolerated for the sake of her child. She knew her vulnerability, and was determined to protect herself from further pain and disillusionment.

'I'm not asking or expecting you to compete with her!' Atreus slammed back at her. 'But I am expecting you to think of what is best for the baby you are carrying. Being a parent is about making sacrifices. It is not about what we want but about what our child needs to thrive.'

Unhappily aware from his words that he was not even able to pretend that she might have gifts equal to Krista's in other fields, Lindy nodded stonily. 'Lecture over? I know all about sacrifices. I spent the first four months of my pregnancy being sick at least once a day. I've lost my figure. My clothes don't fit any more. I get so tired I'm in bed by ten most nights. I can't do physical things I used to take for granted.'

Atreus reached down and closed his hands over hers to tug her upright. 'I get the picture— I was insensitive,' he conceded in a raw, driven undertone. 'But I assumed that you would want to marry me. Was that so arrogant?'

The tears that came so easily to her eyes since she had fallen pregnant almost over-flowed. The appeal in his hot golden gaze went straight to her heart. Angrily blinking back the moisture in her eyes, she lifted a hand and smoothed the stubborn angle of his jaw in a soothing gesture. 'No. If I hadn't been pregnant, if you had asked me six months ago, I would have been ecstatic. But that time has gone, and we can't get it back because every-thing has changed. A divorce would be much more traumatic for our child.'

'I just might make a bloody good husband!' Atreus bit out in furious reproof.

'With the right woman, yes. But that woman,' Lindy framed unsteadily, 'isn't me. I wouldn't fit in. I couldn't be what you want and you'd end up hating me.'

Strong arms banding round her, Atreus stared down into her earnest blue eyes and kissed her with all the unstudied intensity of a man fed-up with talking. Utterly unprepared for that radical change of approach, Lindy quivered in feverish shock from the moist dart and dance of his tongue, her breath catching in her throat as an earthquake of response flooded her all too willing body. He slid a hand below her top, flipped loose her bra and closed his fingers round a firm breast with a growling sound of satisfaction that reverberated through his deep chest. With the fingers of one hand she clung to his shoulder, leaning on him while he stroked her throbbing nipples. Excitement was running amok through her sensation-starved body until her imagination jumped ahead a few minutes, to the moment when she would have to surrender her clothing. The thought of lying on her bed like a beached whale while Atreus became much too closely acquainted with her new barrel-like measurements was sufficient to make Lindy pull hurriedly away from him.

She vanished into the cloakroom at speed, to set her clothing to rights and to tell herself off for acting like a wanton hussy. Was it any wonder that he couldn't recognise the meaning of the word no when she threw it at him?

Dragging herself back out of cover to face him again was a huge challenge, but, pink with embarrassment, Lindy returned to the living room.

Atreus dealt her a slow, sensually assessing look from smouldering dark golden eyes. 'We could finish this dialogue in bed…'

Lindy froze.

'I can't think why you look so shocked. That was where we were heading until you took fright.'

Lindy recognised the tough edge of assurance in his measuring scrutiny and knew that her response had weakened her position. 'I didn't take fright… I just realised that what we were doing was absolutely wrong.'

'How?' Atreus incised aggressively.

'If we're not getting married but we hope to raise a child together we need to forge a new relationship—as friends,' Lindy informed him squarely.

'When I want to drag you off to bed I'm not capable of being your friend, *glikia mou.*'

Outraged by his attitude, when she saw her own as being by far the more reasonable, Lindy snapped, 'Of course you could. You've managed without me for months. You've been out with at least a dozen other women!'

Atreus released his breath in a sharp hiss. 'So that's what I'm paying for?'

Lindy squeezed her hands into fists and prayed for self-control. 'You're not paying for anything, Atreus. I'm not that kind of woman. I'm not trying to settle some stupid score.'

Atreus sent her a glittering glance, fierce pride etched in the sombre set of his handsome features. 'I asked you to marry me. Shouldn't that be enough to clear the decks between us?'

Lindy paled. 'I want what's best for both of us.'

'And you also want me,' he stated with insolent certainty. 'Desire is a healthy basis for marriage but a seriously bad basis for friendship.'

Agonised colour washed to the very roots of Lindy's hair. 'Then we'll have to settle on something in between and learn as we go,' she argued shakily. 'Because if you're serious about wanting to be part of our child's life I'm more than willing to accept you in that role… but not as my husband.'

'When do you next go for a medical check-up?' Atreus shot at her without warning, his dissatisfaction with her unhidden.

'Next week,' she answered tautly.

'Let me know the time and the place now and I'll be there. Without flowers or a proposal,' he added with silken derision.

Lindy lost colour. He was offended. His pride had been hurt. She didn't blame him for feeling as he did. He was a very rich man who had probably been raised from no age at all to see himself as one hell of a marital prize. All his adult life women had been trying to get him to the altar without success. Yet he had offered up his freedom as a sacrifice for the sake of their unborn child and she had dared to reject him. But wasn't that wiser than letting him plunge into a marriage to her in which she was convinced he would end up feeling trapped and hating her? It would have been so easy to say yes, she acknowledged painfully, so easy to simply take him at his word, bury her head in the sand and accept him.

Having arranged their next meeting, Atreus sprang back into his Bugatti. It was a dangerously fast vehicle that she would have nagged him for driving had she been his wife. Of course he would just have given her one of his dark stubborn looks and gone ahead and driven it anyway, she reflected ruefully. Atreus would never be tamed or obedient, and she wasn't sure she would ever find it possible to stop wanting him.

* * *

Ben dropped in for a visit the following evening and told her she was crazy to have turned down Atreus's marriage proposal. 'What the hell were you thinking of?' he demanded in apparent disbelief. 'Now you're going to be saddled with a child, it was the best offer you're ever likely to get!'

Since the day Lindy had told Ben that she was pregnant she had seen a great deal less of him. The possessive attitude he had appeared to develop towards her during her affair with Atreus had vanished. Ben seemed to think that a woman with a child had zero attraction for other men and little chance of meeting a permanent partner. That attitude, added to his aversion to anything to do with pregnancy, had not endeared him to Lindy, who found herself trying pointlessly to suck in her stomach when he was around. It was finally beginning to dawn on her that Ben was very immature.

The weeks that followed marked a new departure in Lindy's relationship with Atreus. He was more distant with her, but much more involved in her life than she had ever dreamt he would be. As he had suggested she took on an assistant to help with the business, and her stress level eased while she worked shorter hours and found it easier to take time off.

Atreus accompanied her to all her medical appointments, and when she was sent for a scan at the nearest hospital he met her there. He was endearingly fascinated by the images of the baby on the monitor, and quite stunned by the news that she was expecting a boy.

Afterwards, he insisted that she dine at his London apartment and that she stayed there for the night. Exhausted by the day she'd had, and in no mood to face the journey home by herself, Lindy agreed and called her assistant, Wendy, to ask her to feed the dogs. Never having visited Atreus's home before, she was very curious, but the huge, airy penthouse apartment with its designer furniture and wide open spaces had an anonymous, impersonal quality that left her cold.

During the meal, Atreus excused himself to

take a phone call, and when he returned, he found Lindy fast asleep in her dining chair.

Lindy wakened in the early hours because she was too warm. Although she could only feel a sheet over her, there was good reason for her high temperature. Instead of putting her in one of his guestrooms Atreus had put her in his bed, with him, and she was clamped to his lean and powerful heat-exuding physique like a second skin.

'Go back to sleep, *mali mou.*' Atreus urged huskily.

A single exploratory shift of position had left Lindy wildly aware of the feel of his aroused body against her own. 'You shouldn't have put me in the same bed as you,' she censured.

'When did you turn into such a prude?'

Avoiding any form of intimacy was her protection, she admitted inwardly. In her mind she was already fantasising about what he might do next, and the burn of long abstinence from such pleasures sat like a hollow ache at the heart of her.

'Stop teasing me,' she urged stiffly.

'Relax, you're safe,' Atreus asserted.

Cut to the bone by that assurance, Lindy sucked in a sustaining breath. Of course she was safe. Why on earth had she thought she might be otherwise? Simple proximity to a female body had caused his arousal. After all, he could hardly find her swollen form sexually appealing. She was amazed he had had an arm round her, and wondered if she had burrowed into him while she slept. After all, he never touched her now in that way when she was awake. There had been no more unexpected kisses, not so much as a flirtatious word out of place.

'No sex outside marriage,' Atreus breathed silkily.

Lindy pushed herself up on one elbow. 'What did you say?'

'Sex is out of the question unless you're prepared to marry me.'

In the dim light creeping round the edges of the curtains he was a dark silhouette against the sheets. Lindy glowered furiously down at him. 'I don't want sex!'

Atreus just laughed.

'I mean it, I…don't…want…sex!' Lindy launched, even louder, her face burning in the darkness.

'Liar,' Atreus murmured softly.

Her teeth gritted. 'I'm not staying in this bed with you!' she announced loftily, lunging at the lamp by the bed to switch it on.

'I know it's very frustrating to be able to look but not touch. And, yes, I do notice how you look at me,' Atreus informed her.

'There are times when I really hate you!' Lindy hissed.

Atreus slid out of bed with fluid grace, reached for the robe lying by the bed and extended it for her use. Lindy clambered out of bed a great deal more slowly than he had. Although she was ready to hate him she had planned to stay in the bed, but his move called her bluff. She was awesomely conscious of her proportions in the sensible bra and panties he had mercifully left her clad in, and almost in tears of mortification at having to expose herself to that extent. Naturally the robe would not close across her stomach.

He showed her into the guestroom next door.

In silence, Lindy cried herself back to sleep in a cold bed. She didn't like his sense of humour. Of course he didn't still want to marry her! But she was cringing at the knowledge that he seemed to have the ability to see through her pretences of being simply pleasant and friendly around him. She felt fat and horrible and deeply unsexy, and she wished she had kept quiet when she'd awoken, so that she could have continued to enjoy lying that close to him again.

There would be no opportunities for such togetherness after the baby was born. Their dealings would become much more detached once their son was in existence. Atreus had a very strong sense of responsibility and he had proved that he was extremely reliable. As soon as he'd realised she was pregnant he had become thoughtful of her comfort and very supportive in every way. But she was already worrying about how they would share their newborn child, and whether it would mean that she had to adjust to being regularly parted from her baby.

Later that morning she was woken up with breakfast on a tray. When Atreus strode in she was happily reflecting that there was a lot to be said for being spoiled, and even more to be said for a man who took the trouble to spoil you.

'I know the baby is due in only a couple of weeks, but I think I should introduce you to my family before our son is born,' he imparted, poised at the foot of the bed, looking impossibly sleek and groomed and gorgeous in a business suit.

Lindy avoided looking at him now for longer than two seconds, because she knew that it was not safe to do so. He could spot lusty admiration at fifty paces and she needed to be more careful. But his invitation to meet his family shook her, and she shrank from the challenge of following heavily in tiny Krista's light and delicate footsteps.

'I don't think I'd be allowed to fly at this stage…'

'Private jet,' he pointed out gently.

Lindy could not think of a ready excuse that he would not shoot down in flames. When Atreus got an idea in his head he was unstoppable. 'Suppose…just suppose I went into labour,' she urged, trying to scare him away from the idea.

'We've got plenty of doctors in Athens,' Atreus responded cheerfully, already resolving to ensure that there was a contingency plan for any emergency…

CHAPTER NINE

DURING the flight Lindy asked Atreus about his family.

'Since my grandfather died my Uncle Patras and Aunt Irinia have become the most important people to me. When I was seven years old, they took me into their home,' Atreus advanced with studied casualness.

'I didn't realise that your parents died while you were still a child.'

'They didn't. My mother was a heroin addict and my father couldn't cope with her and a child. When the social services got involved because I was rarely at school my father's family intervened. Patras and Irinia agreed to bring me up. Their own children were already adults, so it was a considerable sacrifice for them to take on a seven-year-old.'

'A heroin addict?' Lindy repeated, settling shocked and concerned eyes on his lean strong face, for it had never occurred to her that he might not always have enjoyed a happy, privileged and secure background.

'She was an artists' model, famed for her wild bohemian lifestyle. Before he met her my father was an exemplary husband and businessman who never put a foot wrong. But he walked out on his marriage for her and even turned his back on his responsibilities at Dionides Shipping. He never worked again. He lived on his trust fund,' Atreus shared with biting contempt. 'He did marry my mother, but they were too different for it to work.' His handsome mouth twisted. 'I barely remember them, but I do remember the violent arguments and the fact that the house was always full of noisy strangers coming and going at all times of the day and night.'

'It must have taken a lot of guts for your father

to stand by your mother. I suppose he had given up so much to be with her that he felt he had to make the best of things,' Lindy mused.

'That's not the family point of view,' Atreus said drily.

Lindy didn't say that she already knew the family point of view just by watching him and listening to what he had to say and how he said it.

'My father let everyone who ever depended on him down—his first wife, his family, his child, even our employees at Dionides Shipping.'

'Is he dead now?'

'He died in a car crash ten years after my mother died of an overdose. He was a weak, self-indulgent man. He lived abroad and he never made a single attempt to see me again.'

Lindy was heartbroken on his behalf. She could see how deep that final omission and hurt had gone. Indeed, it was obvious to her that Atreus had been taught to be deeply ashamed of both his parents, and she thought that was a cruel burden to give a child to carry

into adolescence and beyond. She now understood why Atreus had once confidently
assured her that he would only marry a woman
from a similar background to his own. But this
awareness only made her marvel at the reality
that, in spite of the undoubted conditioning he
had undergone, he had still asked her to marry
him. What she had just discovered gave her a
whole new view of him and of his marriage
proposal.

When he escorted her into the Dionides
family home, a handsome country mansion
outside Athens, Lindy was elegantly clad in a
terracotta linen dress and matching light
jacket.

'Before we join my relatives, I should warn
you that they are very much shocked by the
fact that we are not even engaged, not to
mention married. I told them that they needed
to move with the times, but I doubt if they
took my advice on board,' Atreus drawled
wryly.

Lindy groaned. 'You have a great sense of

timing. I wouldn't have got off the jet if you'd told me that any sooner.'

'I'm the head of the family and they have excellent manners. No one will be rude,' he told her with some amusement.

But, even though he spoke the truth on that score, Lindy hated every moment of the meeting that followed. The interior of the house had a formal funereal gloom, and an echoing silence that seemed a fitting backdrop for the very reserved group of people waiting to greet them. There were about fifteen people in a big room shaded by lowered blinds. The atmosphere, for all the heat outside, was distinctly chilly and unwelcoming, and Patras and Irinia Dionides were the chilliest of the lot. Eyes were swiftly averted from her pregnant stomach, and the fact that a baby was on the way was never once mentioned.

For that reason when Lindy felt a disturbing tightening sensation in her abdomen she did not dare refer to it. As she sat there, trying not to shift position too often, the tightening gradually reached the level of pain. She began to breathe with care, while making frantic calculations and wondering whether she was having a scare or if it was the real thing. When her nerves couldn't stand the suspense any more, and a gasp escaped her at the strength of a particularly strong contraction, Atreus turned to her with a frown of enquiry.

'I think I might be going into labour,' she whispered as discreetly as she could.

Well, there was nothing discreet about Atreus's reaction to that. In the middle of a conversation he leapt upright, yanked out his phone, stabbed out a number and began speaking in an urgent flood of Greek. Consternation spread like a tidal wave, engulfing the room, and while concentrating on keeping calm Lindy tried to console herself with the reflection that going into labour in front of her hosts would presumably linger longer in family memory than whatever favourable impression Krista Perris had left behind her.

'It is just as well that I reserved a room at a

maternity clinic in case we needed it,' Atreus informed her with decided satisfaction, bending down to lift her off her feet and carry her out of the house to the waiting limousine. 'There's also an excellent obstetrician standing by in readiness for our arrival, *agapi mou.*'

Lindy was impressed, and some of her anxiety ebbed away. 'You really do shine in a crisis, Atreus.'

But little else relating to the birth of their son went as they expected. Lindy was in labour for hours, and she was becoming increasingly tired when the foetal heart monitor revealed that the baby was in distress. She was then whisked off for an emergency Caesarean. But her son was the most beautiful baby she had ever seen, with a shock of black hair and a cry as effective as a fire alarm.

Afterwards, Lindy drifted in and out of an exhausted sleep, still suffering from the effects of the anaesthetic she had had. At one point she opened her eyes and saw Atreus staring down into the crib with one long finger caught in his son's grasp. Caught in the act of appreciating his newborn son, Atreus looked happier than she had ever expected to see him.

'Do you like him?' Lindy whispered with a hint of teasing.

'If you can forgive him for what he's put you through, I certainly can,' Atreus declared, brilliant dark eyes shimmering with strong emotion. 'He's so perfect. Have you seen the size of his fingernails yet? They're tiny—he's like a doll. Do you think he's healthy?'

'He was ten pounds! He's a big baby and of course he's healthy.' Lindy was touched by his concern and enthusiasm but she had to force her eyes to swerve away from him again. Just looking at Atreus could make her heart pound, and she wondered when, if ever, her fascination with him would fade. In comparison to him she was a mess, with her tousled hair and unadorned face. Atreus, on the other hand, looked astonishingly vibrant for a male who had missed a night's sleep. Even with his lean, dark and devastating features adorned by a dark shadow of stubble, his tie missing and his suit crumpled, he looked utterly gorgeous.

Atreus straightened from the crib and spread his arms wide in an emphatic gesture. 'I know already that I want to be able to see him every day. I want to be there when he smiles, takes his first step, says his first word,' he told her, in a tone of urgency that locked her troubled gaze back on him. 'I want to pick him up when he falls over, to hold him, be there for him. All those things are hugely important to me. But if you don't marry me I'm unlikely to ever be that close to my son.'

And, watching Atreus stroke an infinitely tender fingertip down over their baby's little face, Lindy was suddenly powerfully aware that she was no longer the primary focus of his interest.

It was clear that Atreus had fallen passionately in love with his first child. She knew in her bones that he would make a terrific father, driven to give his own child what his father had not given him in terms of time, interest and affection. Surely no one else would ever love their child so much as his own father? How could she deny Atreus and her son the closest possible relationship available to them?

And she was still in love with Atreus, wasn't she? Brooding over the truth that she had tried to avoid, Lindy almost stared a hole in the blank space of wall. When Atreus was in her life she was much happier. Even seeing Atreus on a platonic basis, as she had been for the weeks before the birth, had lifted her spirits a great deal, and his support from the instant she went into labour had been invaluable. Feeling as she did about him, didn't marrying him make sense? And even if their marriage didn't last, at least she would have the consolation that she had tried to make it work.

'All right,' Lindy mumbled sleepily, finally breaking the taut, tension-filled silence.

Atreus closed a lean brown hand over hers. 'All right…what?'

'I'll marry you. But be sure and tell your

family that it was all your idea,' she urged, squirming at the mere concept of meeting his relatives again after her undignified exit from their home the previous afternoon.

His ebony brows drew together as he frowned. 'What made you change your mind?'

'I think our son should have two parents,' Lindy mumbled drowsily. 'You and I both grew up without a father.'

Atreus released her hand. 'Get some sleep, *glikia mou.*'

Her feathery lashes dipped, and then suddenly her eyes flew wide again. 'You'll have to wait until I can get into a decent wedding dress!' she warned him.

They decided to call their son Theodor, which was one of the few names that they both liked, and in a matter of days Theodor had become known as Theo.

Atreus's relatives visited them in the clinic. They were surprisingly animated, and a great deal more likeable after being introduced to the youngest and newest member of the Dionides clan.

As soon as Lindy was fit to travel she and Atreus flew back to London. After a week in Atreus's penthouse apartment, with a nanny to help out, Lindy regained her mobility sufficiently to head back home to her cottage and her dogs. While she was occupying one of the guestrooms in Atreus's apartment she had not felt at home.

Alissa and Elinor had insisted on organising the wedding, and Lindy was glad of their assistance and their company. Atreus, after all, was working very long hours, and within a fortnight of returning to the UK went off on a two-week business trip to Asia. When he visited in between times, he focused all his attention on Theo, but was otherwise cool and distant. Lindy waited in vain for his attitude to warm up. She had naively believed that once she'd agreed to marry him everything would go straight back to the way it had been between them, but it was soon clear that she was very much mistaken in that hope.

As their wedding day drew closer, Lindy became more and more apprehensive. She'd found a beautiful dress, and was relieved that she had regained her figure. Of course she had been fairly active during her pregnancy and had not put on a great deal of weight. She was offered interviews by several celebrity magazines which she turned down. She knew that Atreus loathed that kind of publicity, and saw no reason why she should surrender her privacy purely because she was about to become the wife of a very rich man.

The night before her wedding, Lindy stayed in Alissa and Sergei's fabulous town house. She lay in bed, castigating herself for not having had the courage to tackle Atreus and persuade him to talk to her about feelings he had never once acknowledged he even had. Was he actually suffering from a case of cold feet? Did he regret proposing to her in the first instance? Was he ever going to touch her again? Was he even planning on a normal marriage?

Or was he only marrying her to give Theo his name and gain better access to his son?

Those were the fears tormenting Lindy on the day of her wedding, as it dawned on her that her love might well not be enough to oil the wheels of her marriage. Her mood was not improved by the acknowledgement that she was too much of a coward to force those issues with him lest it provoke the cancellation of the wedding.

Elinor, who was acting as her Matron of Honour, loaned her a fabulous tiara to wear with her veil, while Alissa, her bridesmaid, gave her a gorgeous pair of designer shoes. A sapphire and diamond necklace arrived from Atreus, and it was obvious that Alissa had known in advance about that. It was a magnificent gift, and Lindy put it on and spent some time admiring the glittering jewels in the mirror.

'You're the quietest bride I've ever come across,' Elinor complained. 'Is there something wrong?'

'No, of course there isn't,' Lindy disclaimed hastily.

'It's okay to have doubts and be scared,' Alissa declared cheerfully, giving Lindy's shoulder a gentle squeeze. 'Everyone feels like that. Marriage is such a big step, and you've seen so little of Atreus since you came back from Greece.'

'I didn't realise he would be working so much,' Lindy confided ruefully.

'Sergei and Jasim were exactly the same, but when you're living together you'll find more time for each other.'

'You've had a bumpy courtship,' Elinor pointed out. 'You need to talk about what you both want and expect from your marriage.'

Lindy felt it was easy for Elinor, not knowing all that had happened before, to give advice of that nature when Jasim was so obviously deeply in love with her, his wife, and knew no greater happiness than to make her happy. If Lindy had had the confidence of knowing that Atreus was in love with *her*, she wouldn't have had a single worry in her head. But she strongly suspected that if she asked

Atreus to sit down and talk about their mutual wants and expectations within marriage he would run for the hills....and never come back.

When she walked down the aisle at the church, her heart hammering so loudly in her ears that she felt light-headed, Atreus turned to watch her progress. He treated her to a keen head-to-toe appraisal, taking in the off-the-shoulder wedding gown which faithfully followed her womanly curves and complemented them with its simple, understated design. His stunning eyes gleamed like molten gold, and her mouth ran dry because she knew that look, recognising that irrefutably sexual smoulder in his gaze with a leap of answering response and profound relief.

'You look ravishing,' Atreus told her in a roughened undertone when she drew level with him.

It was the most personal thing he had said to her in weeks, and her bosom swelled with pride. He held her hand, his thumb gently caressing the soft inner skin of her wrist, and while little quivers of growing awareness rippled through her body, her brain tossed out the doom-laden thoughts that had been tormenting her.

The ring on her wedding finger, Lindy accompanied Atreus back down the aisle, a buoyant sense of contentment powering her. They would be great together, she promised herself, and she would work so hard at their marriage. She would be a brilliant wife in every way possible.

Those uplifting ambitions shrieked to a sudden forced halt outside when Lindy, watching as the Dionides security team went toe-to-toe with the paparazzi, noticed an unexpected face in the crush. Eyes widening, she stared at Krista Perris, sheathed in a body-hugging bright scarlet dress and with a tiny feathered fascinator on her blonde head that was the last word in cute frivolity. She looked dazzling, and all the men in her vicinity were sucking in their stomachs and straightening their shoulders in the hope of attracting her attention.

As Lindy slid into the wedding limo, she wasted no time in venting her annoyance. 'What's Krista Perris doing here?' she demanded.

Atreus frowned. 'Why shouldn't she be here? My family and hers have been friendly for many years.'

'I didn't realise that,' Lindy admitted gruffly, already regretting her revealing outburst.

'It would have been unthinkable to remove her name from the guest list, but I'm surprised she decided to attend,' Atreus commented, turning his handsome dark head to take another look at the diminutive blonde, his bold bronzed profile clenching taut. 'She looks very well.'

That was all Atreus had to say to put Lindy's nose out of joint, and Lindy was unable to suppress the thought that it was *her* wedding, *her* day, and that Krista Perris had probably had the joy of being eye-catching, beautiful and the centre of attention every day of her entire life. Although resenting Krista's presence made Lindy feel like a mean, jealous cat, she couldn't help feeling insecure and threatened. She reckoned that Atreus was to blame for her feelings by not being more frank with her—until it occurred to her that she would have felt a great deal worse had he told her that he was in love with Krista. His honesty, she conceded heavily, would only be welcome if he was able to tell her exactly what she wanted to hear. And that comforting conclusion seemed unlikely when she recognised his tension at the slightest reminder of the other woman.

At the reception, held at an exclusive hotel, Lindy caught hold of her little flower girl, Alissa and Sergei's daughter Evelina, before she could run in front of a waiter laden with a tray of glasses. She then paused to check her hair in a huge gilt wall mirror.

'You look pretty,' Evelina piped.

'Thank you,' Lindy was saying with a smile

when, without warning, another face joined hers in the reflection and made her stiffen in sharp disconcertion.

It was Krista Perris, flamboyant as a flame in her red dress and fascinator, a silken swathe of blonde hair framing her intent face as she stared back at Lindy with malicious eyes. 'You're the wrong bride,' she pronounced softly. 'And Atreus and everyone here knows it. He'll never stay with you.'

A split second later Krista had moved on, leaving Lindy temporarily unsure that her cool and derisive indictment had actually been said out loud. But the proof was in the hair which had risen at the nape of her neck and the gooseflesh on her bare arms.

The wrong bride. It was a label that hit Lindy hard. Even so, she hadn't been able to prevent the same thought from occurring to her when she first laid eyes on Krista, whose smooth sophistication and social assurance acted as a perfect mirror for Atreus's own.

Of course Krista hated her, Lindy reasoned,

while the speeches were being made and her mind was free to drift. Guilt was biting deeply into Lindy. Krista and Atreus had been seeing each other and, whether she liked it or not, their relationship had become serious enough for Atreus to consider marriage. Then out of the blue had come the revelation that Atreus had an ex-mistress, pregnant with his child, and Krista's romance had crashed in flames. Naturally Krista was bitter. She must have been hurt, Lindy reflected uneasily, her conscience stinging at the knowledge that her decision not to tell Atreus about her pregnancy was responsible for his breaking up with Krista. How must Krista feel, witnessing Atreus's marriage to another woman when only a couple of months ago Atreus had been Krista's lover?

Lindy had tried not to think about that fact since Theo's birth. Atreus had made it very clear that he had no wish to talk about Krista, and Lindy had felt obligated to respect that embargo. It was not so easy to stay silent now,

at her wedding, where she could see that the
Dionides family and the Perris family were
close friends and that a marriage between
Atreus and Krista would have been hugely
popular.

Be grateful for what you have, not what you
don't have, Lindy scolded herself while Atreus
whirled her round the floor in the opening
dance. But she could not forget the fact that
when Atreus had had a free choice he had rele-
gated her to the background of his life and
kept her a secret. He had never pictured her in
the starring role of bride, or as the mother of
his son. In the end fate had refused him that
freedom of choice.

Later, Lindy watched while Atreus took
Krista onto the dance floor. She noticed heads
turning in the direction of that spectacle, and
heard a buzz of comment spread round the
room. She was watching them too, her heart
in her mouth while she struggled to repress a
dangerous mixture of curiosity, jealousy and
insecurity. Atreus and Krista talked easily,

Krista smiling up at him, laughing and flirting with every look and every flick of her long, glossy hair.

'Stop it,' Elinor whispered, leaning closer to Lindy to admonish her friend. 'I can see you torturing yourself and it's silly. If he had genuinely cared about Krista he would never have married you.'

'I don't think I can make that assumption. Atreus was so determined to do the very best he could for his child. Even before he was born Theo made the scales weigh heavily in my favour,' Lindy shared ruefully. 'Did you see how Atreus's family greeted Krista? Like she was a long-lost daughter.'

'I also saw the women of the family hanging admiringly over Theo when his nanny appeared with him. He's the next generation, and I'd say he's done a very successful job of breaking the ice.'

The ice-breaker was cradled in her arms, black lashes down, like silk fans on his little sleeping face, and Lindy dropped a kiss on her son's satin-smooth brow. When she returned to watching her husband she noticed that the smiles Atreus and Krista had worn had ebbed, and that an intent and serious conversation now appeared to be taking place between them. She quickly looked away again and told herself off very firmly. She was letting nerves and insecurity spoil her wedding day.

Lindy would not let herself mention Krista again. She had not been unaware of Atreus's air of reproof when she had mentioned the heiress earlier that day. After all, she was the wife. Krista was a former girlfriend, and the decent, mature thing to do would be to overlook Krista's nasty comment and be generous. Any desires in that direction, however, were slaughtered by the taunting glance of satisfaction that Krista sent Lindy after she persuaded Atreus to stay with her for a second dance.

Late that night Atreus and Lindy flew by private jet to Greece, with Sausage and Samson travelling with them on pet passports.

Lindy was exhausted and slept for much of the flight, wakening more refreshed for the final stage of their journey. They were heading for Thrazos, the private island which Atreus freely admitted was his favourite place in the world. She had not been fit enough to make the trip after Theo's birth, so Atreus had suggested that they spend their honeymoon there.

When they reached the house on Thrazos Lindy could see very little in the darkness. Somewhere down the hill she could see the sea glimmering in the moonlight as they walked from the helipad onto the terrace surrounding the well-lit villa. Atreus handed Theo to his nanny, and a housekeeper took charge to show them into the nursery.

'Oh, this is lovely,' Lindy commented, having strolled into a big room with natural stone walls and a relaxing décor of chunky wood furniture and pale draperies. Deep windows overlooked the grounds.

'Barring emergencies, we should be able to stay here for about six weeks, *mali mou,*'

Atreus informed her, a brilliant smile curving his mouth as she spun round in surprise. 'Yes, that's why I worked day after day after day last month—so that we could enjoy the longest possible break here on the island.'

'I wish I'd known that. You just seemed so busy…'

'Well, I'm not busy now, *glikia mou*,' her bridegroom said huskily, pushing her hair back off her cheekbones with gentle fingers.

'Have you brought a lot of women here?' The question just leapt off Lindy's tongue.

Atreus dealt her a wry look. 'No.'

'Krista?' Lindy prompted, unable to control her need to know just how deeply enmeshed the Greek woman had been within Atreus's life.

His eyes narrowed. 'Yes, she's been here.'

Even as a chill spread inside Lindy at that confirmation she wished she had not asked that stupid question. She shrugged a shoulder. 'I don't know why I asked.'

'The only woman I want here with me now is my wife,' Atreus intoned, lowering his handsome dark head to taste the pouting pink curve of her full mouth.

The hot, urgent taste of him was as intoxicating as the finest wine, while the pure sexual charge he emanated sent her senses leaping and dancing with eager energy. He scooped her up into his arms and strode down the corridor with her into a large airy bedroom with doors out onto the terrace. He set her down with great care on the edge of the massive bed and crouched down to remove her shoes.

And Lindy thought, though she did not want to think it, *I wonder, did he sleep here with Krista?* He tipped up her reddened lips and took them again with the driving hunger that never failed to set her on fire. After all, it had been so long since he had touched her. There had not been a single kiss or caress, and he had shown no sign of wanting her again until he'd looked at her in the church today. She knew that restraint had been necessary in the first weeks after Theo had been born, but they could have shared other intimacies, could at least have shared a bed occasionally. Yet Atreus, who had a remarkably healthy libido, had kept her at a distance. Why was that? What had lain behind all that uncharacteristic restraint and indifference to her womanly wiles? And as he unzipped her dress she wondered if desire for the other woman had held him back from her. Her heart sank, and the warmth and liquid heat within her faded away as shame washed over her. Was he only making love to her now because he knew she was expecting him to? Would he make comparisons? Wish that…?

In a sudden movement of frantic repudiation Lindy thrust Atreus back from her and sprang to her feet, reaching behind her to zip her dress up. 'I'm sorry, I can't do this…I just can't!' she gasped in stricken recoil.

His darkly handsome features clenching hard, Atreus froze. For an instant he studied her with sombre dark eyes, and then he took a pointed step back from her. Her face flamed.

'That's your prerogative. *Kalinichta*,' he murmured without any expression at all.

Reeling in shock from what she had done, Lindy watched him stride out. Tears welled up with stinging effect and rolled down her cheeks. Why did she have to be so horribly insecure? What madness had possessed her? It was their wedding night and she didn't want to spend it alone. What sort of a start was this to their marriage?

CHAPTER TEN

'I SCREWED up,' Lindy told Theo frankly.

There was a magnificent view from the deep terrace that ran the length of the villa on the seaward side. A glorious roll of orchards and lush green land ran down to the sea, which washed the white sand of the cove far below. Lindy, however, was not rejoicing in the scenery, or the beauty of the day. All her attention was pinned to her son, who was reclining in his baby seat. The little boy was kicking his feet with visibly dwindling energy. In his little blue cotton playsuit he looked extremely cute, and she smiled down at him even though she didn't feel remotely happy just at that moment. The stupidity of her own behaviour had come home to roost; she had stuck a spoke in the wheels of her new marriage and she didn't know what to do about it.

Three weeks had passed since their wedding night, when she had crashed and burned in jealousy, and Atreus was still sleeping in one of his own guestrooms. The only time they actually touched was when they passed Theo between them, or when Atreus believed she might be in danger of falling. The rest of the time she was as untouchable as the carrier of some noxious plague. Rejection, she had learned, didn't motivate Atreus to try harder; it made him keep his distance.

That fact apart, the honeymoon was ironically proving an outstanding success in every other way. Atreus might be treating her like a maiden aunt who required physical support on steep paths or when boarding a boat, but he had spared no effort when it came to entertaining her. The island of Thrazos was hilly and green and ringed by beautiful deserted beaches, and Atreus had willingly shown her over every part of it. There was a fishing village at one end, with a picturesque harbour, and almost every day they set sail there on Atreus's yacht and went off exploring.

Golden day had followed golden day, under a sky that stayed resolutely blue and un-clouded. Sometimes Lindy found it stiflingly hot, and she hogged every bit of shade avail-able, but that same heat seemed to energise Atreus. Out at sea there were breezes to cool her overheated skin, and she thoroughly enjoyed the refreshing swim stops and picnics at secluded sandy coves, so that before long her enthusiasm for sailing almost equalled his own. It infuriated her that even when so much was wrong between them Atreus betrayed not the smallest sense of awkwardness. He was polite, calm, and brilliant company, and she dreaded the evenings when she was most often alone. After dinner, when Theo was tucked up for the night, Atreus often retired to his office to work, and Lindy invariably went to bed first.

She loved the more relaxed lifestyle on the island and lived in casual clothes, only putting on a dress when the sun went down. She had dined royally on local dishes at the taverna down by the harbour. She had sat there below the plane tree on one memorable evening, watching Atreus dance a ceremonial dance with the other men in celebration of a saint's day. The only freedom he had known growing up had been on Thrazos. His over-protective guardians had been happy to see him spend his free time here on the island. It was on Thrazos that Atreus had learned to sail, and he knew everyone in the town by name, pausing to greet people in the narrow streets and ask knowledgeably after their families.

On the yacht they also sailed to more so-phisticated haunts on the island of Rhodes. Atreus had purchased a beautiful set of modern designer jewellery for Lindy in Rhodes Town, and she had shopped in the designer outlets to add to a holiday wardrobe that had turned out to be inadequate for her needs as the days passed. Theo travelled almost everywhere with them. At the end of their first week he had been baptised in a simple but moving ceremony held in the island's church, Ag Roumeli. He was a pack-up-and-parcel baby, happy to sleep or eat anywhere and at any time without complaint, and she found him a pure joy to look after.

Lindy gazed down into her son's big dark eyes. 'I screwed up,' she said again, thinking wretchedly about the wedding night which she had wrecked. 'But your father is very slow on the uptake,' she complained, thinking of all the loaded hints she had dropped since, not one of which had been taken up and acted on.

In an effort to redress the damage she had made several first moves: reaching for his hand, dressing in her most inviting outfits, looking, smiling, striving to flirt...all to no avail. In despair she had even steeled herself to sunbathe topless on the yacht, only to be warned, as she lay there in self-conscious embarrassment, that she was asking to get burned. Either she no longer had what it took to attract Atreus, or only a grovelling apology was going to break the ice.

That evening, when Atreus had gone off to work in his office and Lindy had filled as much time as she could saying goodnight to Theo, who was usually asleep before she was even out of the nursery, she decided that it was time to be more aggressive in her tactics.

Atreus glanced up with level dark eyes full of enquiry when she appeared in the open doorway. 'Something up?'

Lindy could feel colour burrowing up below her skin in a sunburst of heat. She brushed her damp palms shakily down over the skirt of her elegant white sundress and breathed, 'I'm sorry about the way I behaved on our wedding night.'

Arrogant dark head lifting at an angle, Atreus lounged back in his chair and studied her with stunning golden eyes. 'Is that a fact? If that's true, why has it taken this long for you to do something about it?' he countered drily.

Having had to push herself to the brink to make her approach and apology, Lindy wanted to scream in frustration. Atreus was always so contrary. He never managed to do what she expected or wanted him to do. Here she was, trying to bridge the chasm between them, while he chose to take a more hostile stance at the most inopportune moment. 'You didn't say anything, either,' she pointed out helplessly.

'It wasn't my place or my problem. It was for you to speak to me. Something you seem to find very intimidating,' Atreus derided. 'Of course, you did do the exact same thing when you realised you were carrying my child.'

Dismay filled Lindy and she gave him a reproachful glance. 'Don't drag that in as well—that's over and done with!'

'No, it's not. Not when you're still hiding things from me. I find it hard to believe that I used to think you were so open and honest.'

'I was very stupid on our wedding night.' Lindy knotted her hands together as she fumbled for the right words. 'I don't know how to explain it you.'

'You're going to have to find a way, because until you have explained it to my satisfaction I'm not sharing a bed with you again.' Atreus spelt out that assurance without hesitation.

In receipt of that thrown gauntlet, Lindy gritted her teeth. 'You're being horribly unreasonable.'

Atreus sprang upright and strode forward. 'Not at all, I've been generous beyond all expectation,' he returned in hard contradiction. 'Some men might have walked out on you and the marriage on the same night. I stayed and gave you time to work it out. If this is the result after three weeks, I'm not impressed.'

Temper was jumping up and down inside Lindy like hot steam trying to escape. 'Obviously I shouldn't have bothered trying to apologise!'

'It was done with such little grace that it was a waste of your breath,' Atreus conceded, in a far from conciliatory way.

Provoked even more by his cold-blooded calm and scrupulous civility, Lindy was so wound up she was trembling with temper. 'There are times when you can really make me hate you, Atreus, and this is one of them. I was jealous of Krista—there I've told you. Are you happy now?' she demanded fiercely, resenting him for dragging that demeaning truth out of her. 'When you admitted you'd been with her here in this house, and presumably in that same bed, I was scared you'd be comparing us, that you really wanted her and not me… I freaked out, all right?'

Atreus viewed her with steady narrowed eyes and a strong air of frowning disbelief. 'You pushed me away because you were jealous of Krista?' he pressed.

'Of course I was jealous of her!' Lindy slammed back, blue eyes very bright as she lifted and dropped her arms in speaking emphasis of the point. 'How could I not have been jealous? You took her straight to visit your family. I was with you eighteen months and you never took me anywhere near them. Your family love her. She's everything I'm not. You said you wanted a rich wife from the same background as you, and who fits that description more perfectly than Krista Perris?'

'Only on paper.' Atreus was still staring fixedly at her, and in a sudden movement he closed the space between them and pulled her to him, hugging her close to his lean, powerful body in an embrace that left her breathless. He pushed her hair back off her brow in an almost clumsy movement. 'You crazy, crazy woman,' he censured. 'You had no need to be jealous.'

'She's really beautiful,' Lindy reasoned, pain rather than resentment tugging at her uneven voice.

'But it's you I want, *agapi mou,*' he whispered raggedly, brilliant eyes of hot liquid gold scanning her upturned face. 'It's always been you.'

Lindy leant into his strong supportive frame, wanting to believe what he was telling her yet not daring to do so. 'That's so hard to believe.'

Atreus hauled her up against him and tasted her mouth with a burning, driving hunger that left her shivering in delicious quivering surprise. 'Day by day, hour by hour, you've been killing me with your happy smiles and cheerful conversation. I thought you didn't care if we were no longer lovers,' he ground out. 'How was I supposed to work out that you were jealous of Krista?'

'At the wedding Krista told me that I was the wrong bride and that you'd never stay with me,' Lindy shared in a shamed undertone, for even repeating that melodramatic warning mortified her.

Atreus frowned, and swore long and low in Greek. 'You never tell me anything,' he condemned afresh, throwing the ball back in her court.

'I didn't want to run to you and tell tales about Krista…that's so juvenile,' she groaned.

'But if you're juvenile enough to believe that kind of silly nonsense,' Atreus reasoned, with an incredulity he couldn't hide, 'telling me would have been more sensible.'

'For goodness' sake,' Lindy interrupted vehemently. 'I felt guilty about Krista so I didn't want to make a fuss. After all, if I hadn't fallen pregnant you'd still be with her!'

His lean, strong face clenched. 'No, I wouldn't be.'

Silencing her with that unexpected contradiction, Atreus lifted her up into his arms and carried her down to the master bedroom at the end of the corridor.

'Sometimes you drive me insane,' he admitted quietly. 'I didn't know why you behaved that way on our wedding night but I was reluctant to force the issue. I was aware that your main reason for marrying me was Theo. You made that very clear. And I understood. Our marriage was the best solution to his birth—but what about us?'

What about us? It was a question that neither one of them had tackled in advance of their marriage, although they had examined what it would mean for their unborn child from every possible angle. Somehow Lindy had been guilty of just blindly assuming that everything would come right without any specific input from her.

As Atreus settled her down on the wide divan bed, Lindy compressed lips still tingling pleasurably from the pressure of his. 'It's your fault I felt so insecure. You kept me at arm's length before the wedding.'

'You turned me down when I asked you to marry me. How was I supposed to behave?' Atreus framed grimly. 'I didn't know where I stood with you, and the bond we had left felt too fragile to risk for the sake of sex.'

Engaged in kicking off her shoes, Lindy gave him a troubled look at that explanation. 'I had no idea you felt like that. There's only one reason I turned you down—I thought you were only asking me to marry you because you felt it was your duty to do so because I was pregnant. And I didn't want any man on those terms.'

'That's not how I felt, *agapi mou*. But then I didn't really understand what I was feeling until after that point,' Atreus conceded heavily. 'So it's hardly surprising that you had no idea either.'

Lindy stood up and, emboldened by that kiss, slid her arms round his neck. 'I don't like sleeping alone…'

Atreus locked her to his big powerful frame. 'Do you honestly think I do?'

'That night after I had the scan, when you took me to bed with you in your apartment, you wanted me then—'

'And I knew you wanted me. But I wanted something more lasting for us than occasional sex when you were in the mood,' Atreus breathed, unzipping her dress and peeling it down her helpfully extended arms.

Lindy had turned hot pink. 'I'm not that shameless!'

'No?' Atreus nibbled her full lower lip while he dispensed with her bra and moulded her creamy curves.

'All right, I can be. You taught me bad habits,' she muttered, feverishly unbuttoning his shirt and yanking it off him with more haste than cool. 'But occasional wouldn't be enough for me.'

Atreus gazed down at her with sudden unholy amusement, and laughed out loud as he tugged her down on the bed with him. 'I didn't want to end up in some undefined messy relationship with you and my child.'

'So, it was marriage or nothing?' Lindy completed, spreading her fingers over his muscular hair-roughened torso in a wondering caress of reacquaintance. As she let her hands slide wantonly lower, she felt his shudder of response with deep loving satisfaction.

Stripping off the remainder of his clothing, Atreus caught her to him and kissed her with a force of hunger and urgency that told her how much he needed her. 'You made it clear that you were only marrying me for Theo's sake,' he reminded her.

'When did I do that?' she queried, her eyes pools of enquiry as she flopped back breathlessly against the pillows and gloried in the feel of his long, lean body settling over hers.

'After Theo's birth.'

Lindy blinked. 'I forgot about that. You asked me why I'd changed my mind… Theo wasn't the only reason. I was saving face.'

'I didn't know that. I was too much aware of

how much I'd hurt you in letting you go in the first place,' Atreus admitted in a taut undertone.

'Probably only because I told you. You're not exactly on the ball when it comes to other people's emotions.'

The wry hint of a smile momentarily stole the gravity from his face. 'Or even my own.'

Something in the troubled expression of those black-lashed eyes yanked painfully at Lindy's heartstrings, and she stretched up to kiss him. That kiss deepened and strengthened with a passion more powerful than any they had yet experienced together. Conversation was forgotten as more primitive needs drove them. At the instant he entered her wildly responsive body her excitement surged to a burning peak and the explosive heat inside her overflowed, sending ripples of quivering pleasure that left her sobbing his name with delight.

'Now you feel like you're mine again, *yineka mou,*' Atreus said huskily, bestowing a tender kiss on her lush mouth and holding her until the wild pounding of her heart and her thrumming pulses had subsided to a bearable level.

Lindy lay in the blissful togetherness that followed feeling happier and more at peace than she had felt for many, many months. Luxuriating in his proximity, she knew that being close to Atreus again felt like coming home. *It's you I want…it's always been you.* That was all he had had to say to win her back, heart and soul, and of course she wanted to believe every word of that assurance—even though she felt that it would be the ultimate vanity not to accept that he had to be exaggerating.

Stunning golden eyes scanned her preoccupied face. 'What are you thinking about?'

Lindy smiled. She had the perfect answer to that unfamiliar question from his quarter. 'You. Happy now?'

'I'm amazingly in love with you,' Atreus confessed with a ragged edge to his delivery. 'It's the first time I've been in love. It hit me in the face, but I still didn't recognise what it was. I was miserable without you. Nothing felt right any more.'

'You love me?' Lindy repeated in astonishment. 'Since when?'

'Probably the first month we met,' Atreus admitted. 'I wasn't brought up to pay heed to emotions. I was raised to respect a code of head over heart, and it worked like a charm until I met you. I'd fallen in lust, but never in love. I never really cared about a woman until I met you.'

Lindy treated him to a blissful smile. *I was miserable without you.* It was all she needed to hear to forgive the memory of those wretched months without him. 'How miserable were you?' she prompted, wanting every gory detail.

'I didn't like Chantry House without you in it. The place felt flat and empty. I couldn't concentrate at work, and I was so bad-tempered two of my PAs asked for transfers. I missed you so much, and I was totally unprepared for feeling like that. When I let you go,

I decided that it was probably time for me to look for a wife rather than another lover.'

'Why?'

'I'd been so comfortable, so settled with you. Did it never occur to you that we lived together like a married couple on our shared weekends? It was the most stable relationship I'd ever had,' he volunteered. 'But, no matter how many women I met, I couldn't replace you.'

'You found Krista,' she reminded him a shade tartly.

'I didn't need to find Krista. I've known her all my life. I turned to her because she seemed to match that blueprint in my head of the woman I should marry to have the best hope of a successful relationship,' he admitted, tugging Lindy out of bed and into the *en suite* bathroom, where he switched on the shower in the wetroom.

Lindy looked up at him, noting the dark reflective look in his eyes, realising that it was a struggle for him to tell her so much. 'Why did you say she was only perfect on paper?'

His lean, strong face shadowed. 'It was the truth. From the start she courted publicity, which I hated. That's why we visited my family so quickly—because she had ensured they knew we were seeing each other from the first week.'

That information told Lindy that he had not been with Krista anything like as long as she had believed. She stepped beneath the water with him. 'And of course your family was ecstatic.'

'If they'd known as much as I now know about her, they would have been considerably less keen. Krista and I have nothing in common but our backgrounds. She's never worked a day in her life, and doesn't even understand the need for it.'

'That must have been a crash course in compromise for a workaholic like you,' Lindy guessed, slippery with shower gel as he subjected her to a slow, thorough wash. 'But you still brought her here to the island.'

'That was light years back, when we were teenagers. She was only one in a whole crowd of friends who came out here for a party.'

'Oh…I assumed it was much more recent than that,' Lindy faltered as he spun her under the water to rinse her.

'You must be joking. Krista doesn't like a quiet life, or the outdoors. She can't live without shops and clubs, and she thinks sailing is very ageing for the skin,' he completed with suppressed scorn.

Lindy laughed at that news. 'No, I suppose you're right. She definitely wasn't the perfect woman for you.'

'*You* are the perfect woman for me, but I was so stupid I didn't recognise the fact until it was almost too late,' Atreus groaned, wrapping her with care in a big fleecy towel. 'I should have walked away from Krista sooner than I did, but I kept on thinking that eventually I would see something more in her. I didn't sleep with her.'

Anchoring her towel more securely, Lindy stared up at him in bewilderment. 'You… didn't?'

'No. I knew that once I did her expectations

would be roused, and I backed off because I wasn't sure about her. When I saw that newspaper and realised you were pregnant, it hit me very hard…'

'So hard that you flew in with a lawyer to help me make a statement denying that it was your child!' Lindy tossed back.

'I was angry, and jealous that you were carrying what I believed to be another man's baby. It never crossed my mind that the child might be mine. We had been apart almost five months at that point,' Atreus reminded her, linking a towel round his lean hips as he uncorked a bottle of wine from a cabinet in the bedroom and filled two glasses with pale liquid.

'I'm sorry I didn't come and tell you that you were going to be a father when I found out myself.' Lindy sighed guiltily. 'I can see how much it complicated everything. You had to tell Krista and break up with her—'

'That's not how it happened,' Atreus cut in, pressing a button that made the glass doors slide back, enabling them to walk out onto the sun-drenched patio beyond that overlooked the grounds.

Lindy sipped her wine. 'How did it happen?'

'I went to see Krista to end the relationship and tell her about you,' he admitted levelly. 'The maid assumed I was expected and let me into Krista's apartment, where I found her and a selection of her friends enjoying a cocaine party.'

Lindy froze, and stared at him in consternation.

'I'd often found her very moody, and I was blind not to suspect that drugs were involved. I'm fiercely anti them,' Atreus breathed grimly. 'That was the moment that it hit me in the face—I had let the love of my life walk away and had then wasted my time trying to idealise a woman who couldn't hold a candle to you. I was ashamed I could be so out of touch with my own feelings that I hadn't even appreciated that what I felt you was love and respect and friendship, and all the other things that a successful marriage needs to thrive. I had it all and threw it away!'

Shocked as much by what he had told her

about Krista as by being told that he loved her, Lindy set her glass down and wrapped her arms round him. 'No, you didn't. I started asking questions and you just weren't ready for that. It all blew up in our faces.'

Atreus dealt her a rueful appraisal and gripped her hands hard in his. 'Don't be kind to make me feel better. I don't deserve to feel better on that score. You had to leave for me to appreciate you, and if I'd lost you for ever I would only have had myself to blame for it.'

'Do Krista's family know about the drugs?' Lindy asked awkwardly.

'When I saw her at the wedding she promised to tell them, because she needs to go into rehab.'

'Was that what you were talking about when you both looked so serious?'

'I know that once she tells her family she'll get the support she needs. If she doesn't, I'll do it for her. Now, can we talk about us instead of Krista?'

Her eyes softened. 'Of course.'

'Thankfully,' Atreus murmured, dark golden

eyes clinging to her animated face with warm appreciation, 'I got a second chance with you through Theo being conceived. And second time around I'd learned what I needed to know. I knew exactly what I wanted and what I was fighting for—your love.'

A rueful laugh fell from Lindy's lips. 'You never lost my love. There were weeks when I thought a lot of bad, unforgiving thoughts about you, but I still loved you underneath.'

Atreus sank down on the sofa on the patio and scooped her onto his lap. 'And…now?' he queried tautly.

Lindy helped herself to his wine, because her own glass was out of reach, and kissed him with joyous abandon. 'Can't you tell how I feel? I'm crazy about you.'

'Crazy enough to apologise…'

'You wanted to make me grovel!' she condemned.

'It was the fate you deserved,' Atreus told her. 'I was devastated when you pushed me away on our wedding night, *agapi mou.*'

Her eyes stung with sudden ready tears of remorse, for she could tell by his voice that he had indeed been knocked back hard by her rejection. She kissed him again, more than willing to make up for that mistake. They became entangled on the sofa, and as things heated up they headed back indoors to the comfort of their bed, where they made love, exchanged lovers' promises and jokes, and lay together feeling very blessed to have found each other…

Almost three years later, Atreus and Lindy hosted a weekend party on Thrazos, to celebrate their third wedding anniversary.

Sergei and Alissa had sailed in on their latest yacht, *Platinum II*, and Atreus and Lindy, Jasim and Elinor had been given the full tour of the fabulous brand-new craft. The men had stayed onboard longer than the women and children, while Atreus had manfully withstood Sergei's teasing about his own small craft, saying that he had to be the only Greek shipping tycoon alive without a huge yacht.

'I hope Atreus doesn't go off and buy a bigger yacht now. You wouldn't believe how competitive men are about them,' Alissa lamented. 'I bet you anything that if Atreus does buy one it'll be larger than *Platinum II*.'

'I don't think so. Atreus likes to sail a yacht single-handed. If he bought anything bigger than what he has now, he would need to take a crew out with him. He also likes speed, and sometimes races her.'

'I can see Sergei liking that,' Alissa quipped with a grin. 'I might like it too—more exciting than football.'

Well aware that Alissa was not over-enamoured of her husband's favourite sport, or his ownership of a football club, Lindy laughed. 'But it's much more dangerous,' she warned.

Children were chasing round the villa, hotly pursued by their nannies and Samson, Sausage and Alissa's dog, scruffy little Mattie. Lindy bustled about, checking that everyone had what they needed to be comfortable, but she did not have much to do because their house-keeper was so very efficient.

Soon they took the children outside, to let them burn off their energy. Elinor's three kids, Sami, Mariyah and little Tarif, were in-separable from Alissa's two, Evelina and Alek, and Theo fitted right in. Tall for his age, like Alek, and also a daredevil, he raced about on sturdy legs. Prince Sami, the eldest and now the direct heir to the throne of Quaram, was undeniably the leader of the group. Mature for his years, he was already demonstrating the social skills he had begun learning from the moment his father, Jasim, became King of Quaram, when his grandfather, Akil, had passed away.

'They're such great company for each other,' Elinor pronounced with satisfaction. 'If the children are fully occupied we get to spend more time together.'

'You're pale, Lindy,' Alissa remarked anx-iously as their hostess supervised the arrival of a tray of cool drinks. 'Let me take care of that. You've been very busy today and you should sit down.'

'I'm fine…it's the heat.' Lindy settled heavily into an armchair, stretched out her legs and tried to relax. She was six months pregnant with twins, and as far as she knew both were girls. Theo couldn't wait for them to be born, and Lindy was already looking forward to the prospect of doing girlie things with her daughters and choosing pretty clothes.

They dined in state that evening on *Platinum II*. It was a wonderful meal, blessed by a lot of laughter and solid friendship, but by late evening Lindy was glad to walk back into the peace and comfort of their own bedroom.

Atreus eased her down on the bed and thoughtfully flipped off her high heels for her.

'Happy anniversary, *agapi mou*,' he murmured, sliding a jewellery box into her hand.

'It's not until tomorrow,' Lindy reminded him.

'But tomorrow we will have company, and tonight we're alone.' Atreus flicked open the box for her and removed a gold bracelet hung with charms.

Her interest quickened as she realised that the dainty charms had been selected to have relevance to her life. There was a little boy with a football, a big dog and a little dog, a racing yacht, a tiny island, and a cat—which revealed that Atreus had noticed the scrawny feral moggy she had smuggled into the house after all. But most precious of all was the diamond heart charm etched with her husband's name.

'My heart in your hands,' Atreus told her, his eyes brilliant with emotion as he framed her smiling face with caressing fingers. 'I want to thank you for the gift of three wonderful years and a child I adore…not to mention the two on the way…'

'Yes, we've done very well on the family front,' Lindy whispered, all her attention locked to his lean, dark, devastatingly handsome profile as he clasped the bracelet on her wrist. 'But the most important thing is that you make me feel incredibly happy and valued. That's why I love you so much.'

'The longer you're with me, the more I love you, *agapi mou,*' Atreus intoned, bending his dark head to steal a passionate kiss that shimmied through her nerve-endings like a delicious wake-up call. 'And I'm never going to stop loving you.'

Her trust complete, she locked her arms round him as best she could with her tummy in the way. With a sound of amusement low in his throat, he rearranged her on the bed for greater comfort, and smoothed a loving hand over the swell of her stomach. 'You're beautiful,' he told her softly.

And she knew that in his eyes she was. Her happiness knew no bounds. 'We're together for ever,' she told him lovingly.

With his next kiss he sealed the deal.

MILLS & BOON PUBLISH EIGHT LARGE PRINT TITLES A MONTH. THESE ARE THE EIGHT TITLES FOR JULY 2010.

GREEK TYCOON,
INEXPERIENCED MISTRESS
Lynne Graham

THE MASTER'S MISTRESS
Carole Mortimer

THE ANDREOU
MARRIAGE ARRANGEMENT
Helen Bianchin

UNTAMED ITALIAN,
BLACKMAILED INNOCENT
Jacqueline Baird

OUTBACK BACHELOR
Margaret Way

THE CATTLEMAN'S ADOPTED FAMILY
Barbara Hannay

OH-SO-SENSIBLE SECRETARY
Jessica Hart

HOUSEKEEPER'S HAPPY-EVER-AFTER
Fiona Harper

MILLS & BOON PUBLISH EIGHT LARGE PRINT TITLES A MONTH. THESE ARE THE EIGHT TITLES FOR AUGUST 2010.

THE ITALIAN DUKE'S VIRGIN MISTRESS
Penny Jordan

THE BILLIONAIRE'S HOUSEKEEPER MISTRESS
Emma Darcy

BROODING BILLIONAIRE, IMPOVERISHED PRINCESS
Robyn Donald

THE GREEK TYCOON'S ACHILLES HEEL
Lucy Gordon

ACCIDENTALLY THE SHEIKH'S WIFE
Barbara McMahon

MARRYING THE SCARRED SHEIKH
Barbara McMahon

MILLIONAIRE DAD'S SOS
Ally Blake

HER LONE COWBOY
Donna Alward